T0149363

AND THEN THERE WERE FIVE

AND THEN THERE WERE FIVE

A Circle of Power

Norm O'Banyon

AND THEN THERE WERE FIVE
A CIRCLE OF POWER

Revised Standard Version of the Bible, copyright ©1952 [2nd edition, 1971] by the Division of Christian Education of the National Council of the Churches of Christ in the United States of America. Used by permission. All rights reserved.

This is a work of fiction. All of the characters, names, incidents, organizations, and dialogue in this novel are either the products of the author's imagination or are used fictitiously.

iUniverse books may be ordered through booksellers or by contacting:

iUniverse
1663 Liberty Drive
Bloomington, IN 47403
www.iuniverse.com
1-800-Authors (1-800-288-4677)

ISBN: 978-1-5320-1996-8 (sc)
ISBN: 978-1-5320-1997-5 (e)

Print information available on the last page.

iUniverse rev. date: 03/24/2017

My birth certificate says that I was born in Everett Washington, May 3rd 1973. I'll have to take its word for it. I don't recall much of the early days except a whole bunch of shouting and swearing, a little sister who caused a lot of the trouble and a littler brother who was always trying to hide from it. Did I have a happy normal family growing up? Not even close! With an overworked dad, an irresponsible mom and three untrained, unguided, unwanted kids, there were five, a prime number.

When I was in the sixth grade mom's wandering eye was too much for dad, so he dumped her and I went with him to Bellingham for a new job at Maritime Marine Products. We had a much better place to live. It was an apartment right on the dock where I could fish and catch crabs. As I recall it, dad did the best job he could, working long hours in the summer time and trying to be a single parent. I don't recall him having any girlfriends, just a lot of work and cooking the same darned meals over and over. The good thing about spaghetti or beef stew is the leftovers. Once the meal was made we could feed on it for several days. Cereal for breakfast, peanut butter sandwiches for lunch and left over's for dinner, that's what I remember.

The year before High school, dad's company offered him a better job in Long Beach California. I was happy that he accepted it and we moved from the marina apartment to a little house close enough that I could walk to school. Probably the two outstanding memories I have there is the wrestling team that gave me an early foundation in aggressive contact and the ROTC program that opened the door for my enlistment. When the Cabrillo High School class of 1993 graduated I was eager to be Camp Pendleton bound and my days of the USMC.

What do I remember most of basic training? Let me see. I think I would say the food. There were always great meals! In high school I had wrestled in the 165 pound class, which was a little light for my 5' 11" frame. But all of a sudden I was 195 and solid as a brick. It only took a couple run-ins with my fellow recruits to understand that I was not someone they wanted to mess with. I sent two of them to the infirmary, which demonstrated to my DI (drill instructor) that I could be sent to Quantico for specialized training in advanced hand to hand combat and information gathering. I didn't know it, but that is the beginning of the military clandestine cover. My records show that I was sent to Huntsville Texas to prison for drug trafficking, which of course was illusion. After another sixteen week language course, I was placed in a Special Forces MST (mobile strike team) on Coronado Island in San Diego, with the rank of Warrant Officer (WO). Curiously it was my lack of tattoos that kept me from being easily recognized. Hell, after no shave or haircut for half a year, I hardly recognized myself. My final formal training was in bomb making and knife fighting. That was the scariest because it was so personal and lethal.

Our first few assignments were efficient in taking down small systems in Tijuana and then another in Arizona. In Texas, one of our team was targeted and killed by a drug lieutenant who thought he was invincible. It took us two months to locate him and several henchmen in a bunker. We blew them and about six million dollars worth of their white death into another dimension. I hardly considered the morality of the street justice we used but the retrieval of a field pack full of $100 bills made it easy to overlook. My only regret was in our lack of getting to the organizational leadership. We cut off the snake, but the head was still in business. We had to go to Guadalupe, west of Monterrey Mexico to finish the job. Using the heavy smoke of a calculated brush fire as a cover distraction, we hit the building with a full assault. We wanted to make sure that the snake and his cronies were dead. Several pounds of C4 and their propane tank turned the cocaine headquarters into a crater. There is no way to know how much cash was incinerated, or how much we were able to carry back to cover our expenses. Ethics is a difficult subject. I was given a WO 2 rating.

Our commander, Lt. Colonel Paris Sherman, was so satisfied with that covert operation we were sent on three more Mexican hunting trips and one in Jamaica, each with devastating success and lucrative return. My savings account was impressive. You know, if small amounts of cash are deposited in different banks, no one seems to pay attention to the conduct of a grubby street bum. By then I was a WO 3.

Perhaps that fact allowed Mr. Sherman to open a new level of war against drugs. I became a solo operative. As a street bum, I could hunt in the shadows of the city where drug activity was known to take place. Taking my time to identify a target, I could push my cart nearby without any concern. I could even ask them for a handout. Once I located their operation, it was just a matter of choosing an attack opportunity, usually just before dawn. I limited my targets to four opponents. A knife is silent, lethal and reusable with no trace. After overpowering the targets, I removed the available cash and set a cover fire. The news media almost always blamed the scene on gang activity. I lost count of how many I accomplished.

Mr. Sherman was reassigned to the Pentagon and Lt. Colonel Dwight Blakely replaced him with a completely different understanding of our purpose. There would be no operations on foreign soil and most definitely no domestic operation without warrants and due process. Our MST was broken up and I was the only remaining NCO. LT. Col. Blakely assigned me to port surveillance, which meant wandering around acres of containers in the hopes of stumbling on criminal activity. My weekly reports failed to mention the solo war on dealers that I continued surreptitiously. I visited the ports of San Pedro, Los Angeles, San Francisco, and

Seattle. As long as I was in the Pacific Northwest I thought I'd look up my family. Regrettably I could only find my little brother. The information I had was that he was a high school teacher, but I found him as a custodian at an AIDS clinic. I hardly recognized him and I'm sure he didn't know who I was.

"Good morning Mr. Winter. What's this?" Lt. Col. Blakely asked the clean shaven officer in uniform before him.

"The top one you will recognize as another weekly report. I found no irregularities in the Port of Seattle, although I found it to be a beautiful one, sir." Michael took a breath and continued, "The second one is a request for separation, sir."

"What?" the startled officer said. "Why in the world would you request separation with only six years to reach retirement?" The reality of the request dawned on him. Without this Warrant Officer, he would have no command. "May I sweeten the moment by asking if another pay-grade would change your mind?"

"No, sir it would not. I'm afraid the nature of this mission is an enormous waste of time. Six more years of it would be intolerable to me. I have applied for an interview with Secret Service where three of our former Warrants have relocated."

In a plaintive voice his commanding officer asked, "Is there anything I can offer you to change your mind?"

"No sir." Michael said, feeling a bit sorry for this officer who was so out of touch with his mission.

A few minutes later he called the number he had been saving. "Hey, Randall its Michael Winter." He listened and then with a smile, he said, "Yeah I miss you guys too." He listened and responded, "No, there are no missions only walking the docks all over the place. I feel like a damned night watchman." "Yeah that's why I'm calling. I have requested separation papers and an interview with the service." He listened again. "You think there is a waiting list just for the interview?"

"Michael, brother there are hundreds of applications, and while not one is your caliber, the starting level is pretty crappy. But as long as you are looking, I have another suggestion. There is an agent in LA who called me yesterday. She sounds desperate for a quality personal security and flashed a lot of green for the job. Even if it is just for a little while, I'll bet she would welcome you. Here's the number." They talked a bit more as good friends might and then Michael called the agent.

After a brief introduction the agent asked him, "Were you in the military, Mr. Winter?"

"I've just applied for my separation papers, ma'am," he answered cheerfully.

"Are you trained in combat or self protection?" It seemed she didn't know quite how to ask about his talents as a security guard. "Are you pretty good at self defense?"

"No ma'am. I'm not good, I am the best." He said softly.

There was a long pause and she asked, "How long will it take for you to get here to my office?"

"I believe I can be there in forty minutes, ma'am. Is there a helo pad nearby?"

"Why yes, the Stratton Hotel is right next door." Her voice was questioning.

"Tell me your office number. I'm on my way."

The chopper crew didn't have confirmation for the emergency flight to LA, but at his authorization they hurried on their way. Thirty seven minutes later he walked into Mrs. Scott's office and introduced himself.

"Mr. Winter, you told me you were calling from San Diego," she said in disbelief.

"Yes ma'am," he replied with a smile. The Huey was all ready for a flight to Pendleton. They just brought me a little further."

"I'm impressed. And you said you are the best security guard?" she asked off-hand."

"Yes ma'am, I did." Michael suddenly felt on guard.

The inner door to her office opened and two men stepped in threateningly. The agent said with a frown, "These men believe they are the best. What do you think we should do about that?" He could tell that she was not joking.

Ma'am, this is a very bad mistake. I don't want to hurt these men just to prove a point." The two were circling Michael and he was convinced that he had no choice. "Gentlemen, this is not necessary."

Before he had finished the words, the one on his left charged. He was strong but not quick. Michael turned slightly and drove the side of his foot against the man's knee. A sickening pop and scream were simultaneous. The short chopping strike to the side of his head drove him to the floor unconscious. The second attack came at him high. The strike was blocked and Michael delivered a chopping blade strike to his throat. The gagging man was grasped by a handful of hair and his face was slammed on Mrs. Scott's desk. He slumped unconscious to the floor as well. Perhaps three seconds had passed.

Michael turned and walked out off the office saying, "Lady, you are the dumbest bitch I have ever met." He headed for the elevator pondering how he would get back to San Diego.

"Mr. Winter please wait! Please!" She was running to catch up with him. "Wait please! I didn't know how else to get the best."

"Furiously Michael turned and asked, "What is this, your little private Gladiator test? I could have killed both of those men, you sick son o.." he turned back toward the elevator.

"Her life is in danger at this moment," the agent blurted. "I didn't know what else to do!" She was crying and trying to speak. "You can hate me, but please help her. She's hiding at my place." Her pleading voice cut through his anger.

Michael turned and said brusquely, "Who's in danger?"

Her name is Noell Ferraris. She is married to the director Heinrik Ferraris. He has been a real mean bastard with no scruples and she filed for divorce. He has vowed she won't live to spend a dime of his money. They have twin girls and an older boy. Please help her." Mrs.

Scott's composure was returning. "Today, money is no object. We just must keep them safe. I'm sure he will find her soon."

Michael stepped back toward her and said, "Call an aid car for those guys and let's go. I can't help her from here."

Mrs. Scott nodded and within moments they were in her car. After several silent minutes she said respectfully, "You are trained. I've never seen such response."

"Yes I am," Michael almost whispered. "It was not in Hollywood stunt stuff."

They wound their way into the Pasadena Hills. Finally on a quiet street she pulled into a driveway and then an open garage. They hurried inside as the door closed.

"Noell," she called. "Noell, its Renee. I've brought security." They heard a door in the upstairs open and footsteps. Four frightened people joined them, while Michael was closing curtains and drapes.

"Noell, this is Michael Winter. In the last few minutes he has convinced me that he is the best to keep you safe."

The slight woman held out her hand in greeting. Michael was impressed with her calm demeanor. If she was in danger, there certainly was no sign of that on the surface. "Let's begin by getting rid of any electronic trace of you all. Will you take the batteries out of your cell phones and any toy or game?" They hurried away to do that.

Michael said to Mrs. Scott, "We're going to need someplace more defendable than this house. We need a bunker. How about making a reservation somewhere down in Oceanside, the closer to the beach the better. I can have support by tomorrow evening." He thought for a moment then asked, "Do you have any weapons in the house?' She shook her head. Michael went into the kitchen and selected two good blades to sharpen. Noell and the children returned and she reported that all of the batteries had been removed.

Michael said in a reassuring voice, "We don't know if they know you are here, but for safety sake, let's assume that they do. It will be best if you all can stay in one room upstairs, in the center of the house if possible. I'll take care of down here. Please do not turn on any lights that would show someone where you are. Finally," he had a big smile, "I'm going to do a better job if I know your names."

Noell was quick to say, "This is my brave son Caleb, who is eight years old and the twins are Celia and Camilla. They are six and will be in the first grade"

Michael carefully shook their hands and complimented their courage. "I think any guests will be here soon if they know you are here. If not, we may take a very late night drive down to Coronado Island, where I am sure you will be safe. In any event, if you hear noises, please do not scream. Sneaky people sometimes try to fool you into revealing where you are hiding."

Shadows filled the house and then darkness. The house was silent and Michael thought they might have done this planning for nothing, and then he saw the green flicker of a night-vision lens, and another. He positioned his attack point and waited. It took them longer than he expected to get the lock open. As two shadow forms entered, Michael turned on the lights. For an instant the attackers were blinded. That was all the time he needed for a heart thrust for one and a slashed throat for the other. Hardly a rustle of sound was heard. He turned off the lights again.

He could hear the faint sound of an ear bud. He found and extracted the device. There was an urgent voice requesting status. He was speaking French. Michael felt like it was military trained, but not very well. Then he heard a car engine start and move away. After about a half hour he carefully cleaned and replaced the knives. He went upstairs and asked the group to carefully come down to the garage in the dark so they wouldn't see the mess he had made. He suggested that they all get in the Escalade. Then Renee could call the police as soon as they were gone.

"You're not going to leave me here with this!" she said bluntly. "They may just come back for me."

Michael said, "Then come along, but call the police anyway. They need to know that an attempt was made here, a very carefully planned attempt. Explain that you are going into hiding for your safety and will contact them tomorrow." She nodded.

It was a little after midnight when he stopped at the Coronado guard station. He showed his ID and reported, "Two adult females and three children to building nine."

In just a minute the guard saluted and said, "Rooms six and seven are available sir." Michael returned the salute and pulled onto the base. He could finally relax. They were safe for sure here.

Michael knew they were confused and frightened so he said lightly, "This is courtesy housing for family visits, usually wives for a conjugal weekend." He chuckled, "this being Thursday it should be pretty quiet." Then in a much more serious tone he said, "We have help on the way. They should be here by noon. Renee did you make reservations?"

The agent nodded with a frown. "I did, at The Spanish Inn, but what's it for?"

"Listen," Michael snapped, "I don't have time to explain every detail to you. You will do what I tell you or you can find someone else. This isn't a game." He softened a bit. "Last night should have shown you that your fears are well founded. Those were well equipped professionals. We have no idea how many more there might be, so we want to get them to come at us in a place of our choosing. Hopefully you will only be here one more night. Then this trouble will be over. Until then you must make no phone calls to anyone. Let's assume that your phones have been tapped." Then as an added thought he said, "Except you Renee. You can call your office to inform them that you are in rooms at the Spanish Inn."

As he pulled up to an attractive building he said finally, "There will be a breakfast tray brought to your room at 0800. If you need anything from the PX, ask the person who brings your tray to provide a courtesy guide. But for God's sake try to remember how much trouble you are in. Don't be dumb." His hard glance at Renee gave her a shiver. Before he left them, he asked Noell about her home, its address, security, general doors and windows. She gave him the security code for the front gate and door to the house. "Does your husband have a panic room or vault?" She nodded and explained how it worked.

Finally he tried to comfort her. "This mess must be terrible for you and the kids. I'm pretty sure it is going to work out O.K. Just know that here and now, you are safe. Nothing can harm you here."

She sobbed a thank you and clung to him. "He is a very wicked man, Michael. I have come to realize that there is no end to his meanness." He was aware of her fragile warm body. In a whisper, she said, "Please stop him from hurting us."

Randall and Denny, another former MTS, arrived about 1400. The three had a short briefing and set about placing enough armament in the Escalade to meet the challenge. They made one tour of the Spanish Inn parking lot and saw nothing suspicious, so they parked where the Escalade could be easily sighted. Michael reminded them to wear the latex gloves so there would be no finger prints. Randall and Denny went to the back of the building to check out the loading dock. Michael went in to register. The desk clerk said, "Really? John Smith?"

Michael produced a California driver's license which verified the name. "My folks thought it was cute, but it is a pain every time I use the damned thing."

The sun was setting when Denny's voice over the ear buds announced that two Range Rovers just parked behind the Cad. Five men in dark clothes were on their way in. Before they reached the lobby the lookout that had remained with the vehicles heard a high voice calling, "Here Angel!" "Angel come!" There was some whistling for a dog. The lookout saw a dark skin man wearing a gaudy floral shirt approaching. He was carrying a baby blanket. "Hey, mister," he said in a high voice, "have you seen my Angel? She's,…." He was near the back of the car. "Oh there you are sweetie." The lookout turned his head to see. It was a careless mistake. The baby blanket concealed a .22 hollow point with a silencer. The gun shot was little more than a hiss and the man was dead before his body hit the ground. "One down," he spoke over the transmitter. He moved the body into the back of the Rover and drove it to the loading dock. That information was also conveyed.

One by one the assailants were separated and eliminated. It was Michael's intent to do that as carefully as possible, leaving no blood trace. Using a laundry cart, the bodies were moved to the loading dock and into a Rover. By midnight the two Range Rovers and the Cadillac moved onto the Hollywood Hills street of celebrity homes. One of which was Heinrik Ferraris'.

There was no sign of movement in the house, which was all dark. "There are three doors with key pads," Michael informed them. "Let's each take one and see if anyone is home." He told them the sequence. Randall went in the front door, carefully. As he stepped into the darkness powerful hands grasped him and a wrestling contest began. The bodyguard was stronger but not more talented than Randall. But finally a strong arm wrapped around his face and the end seemed eminent. At that moment an ice pick entered the big man's ear canal and thrust into his brain. His limp body was eased to the floor. No other guards seemed to be there.

"Damn, I hate it when you do that," Randall growled. "But damn it sure works."

"Let's make sure we are alone. Turn on the lights in every room. There is a panic room that we'll do last." It only took a few minutes to determine that the house was clear. Michael said, "O.K. final scene. Denny go out to the Cad and bring that gas grenade. I do believe that will do it."

Michael tapped in the code and the heavy door popped open a crack. Instantly a heavy pistol report sounded. Michael pulled the pin on the grenade and tossed it into the secret room. He slammed the door closed to make sure it was sealed. They didn't feel the detonation or smell the gas that had a four minute efficiency cycle. "While we wait, let's get those bodies out of the Rovers and into the pool."

When Michael reopened the panic room there was no resistance, Heinrik's body was motionless. Michael sat him in the chair there, felt for a pulse and when there was none he made sure with an application of the ice pick. He retrieved the gas canister and made sure the pistol was in the dead man's hand.

"Good job guys," Michael said finally. "I think it is time to go home. Denny get the Cad started. I'll call 911 to report an invasion."

Four minutes later the police found the bodies of seven foreign nationals in the pool and the lifeless body of the home owner locked in his panic room with no visible wounds and the only GSR (gunshot residue) was on his hands.

A bit after 0900, Michael knocked on their door. It was opened by Renee, but Noell asked first, "Is it over?" Her voice was small, afraid of the answer in either case.

"Yes ma'am, it is definitely over. I believe you would not want to hear the details. But let me assure you that your home was not damaged in the least. I think they may be draining the pool today, but that is inconsequential. I will drive you both home if you choose, or you can spend one more day here in solitude." Looking at Mrs. Scott, he said, "You might want to call the police for advice. You have been in seclusion and have no idea what events have happened in your absence." It was as near to a suggestion as he wanted to go.

Then looking at the children he said, "I am so proud of how brave and obedient you all were last night. Oooowee, that was scary and you were just as brave as super heroes." He reached over and ruffled Caleb's hair. "Caleb the bold! Then the twins "Celia, the courageous and Camilla the undaunted. That's what your names mean as far as I'm concerned. I couldn't be more proud of you all." No one smiled more warmly than their mom. That may have been a first for her kids; they rarely received honest praise like that.

Mrs. Scott's phone call may have been the most lengthy. "Yes, sir," she explained for the third time. "I was interviewing Mr. Winter for a security job when I learned that Mrs. Noell Ferraris was at my house seeking shelter from her angry husband. When we got to my house there was a terrible mess and Mr. Winter took us to Coronado Island, where he gave us shelter for the night." "That's right sir, we have been here for 36 hours. You can check with the gate security. We have not left. No sir," I don't know anything about bodies in my kitchen or the Ferraris'. No sir. May I have it cleaned so I can return home? Thank you sir."

The first half of the drive home had been pretty quiet. Finally, Mrs. Scott asked, "Michael what would you think if I could get you a steady cadre of security positions. They would pay very generously." She waited for a positive response.

"And how much would you accept for this generous service?" he asked in a pretty cheery voice,

"My usual fee is 35% for security jobs, but for you I'd do 25%. She felt like that was a good deal.

He was just about to tell her where she could put her 25% when Noell said quietly, "I've wanted to ask you a similar question, but I'm afraid you will say, 'No'." She looked at him with admiration and a twinge of fear. She had never known someone like Michael. "I'm going to need someone to protect me and the children in the coming months. Everybody is going to be after his investments, his holdings, everything. Attorneys will be sharpening their pencils to work me over. Will you consider $10K per month and the use of the guest cottage and any car in the garage? You may even dine with us if you like."

He tried to keep a disinterested face, even though that offer was at least double what the Secret Service was paying. "What would your expectations be?"

"I don't know. We could work that out. Today I know what it feels like to be safe. I want more of it for me and my children. I would like you to attend meetings with me where decisions are being made. I'm not the brightest crayon, as they say. Protect me from those who would take advantage." Noell's eyes held his and she didn't blink.

Finally he cracked a bit of a smile and said, "It seems my calendar is pretty clear right now. I'll agree to a test month. It will probably take that long for the police to complete their investigation."

Renee asked, "will you accept a thousand dollars for the two days you have given me?' When Michael's cold eyes gave her a long stare, she added, "I mean a thousand for each of you. I'm thinking if Noell gets you, Randall and Denny may accept my proposal."

"If that is what you think is fair payment," Michael said softly, "for saving your lives and taking out nine adversaries, I want you to forget my phone number and get ready to hear some new words from Randall and Denny. They may want to come to LA and start their own agency."

"Then what would you think a fair pri…" she was interrupted by a growl.

"Are you kidding me lady? There is no fair price for what has happened in the last thirty six hours," Michael said brusquely. "Give us whatever you want. But know that you have received a remarkable gift." He was quiet for the remainder of the trip.

They retrieved their cell phones and other devices from the agent's home and Michael placed three heavy carrying bags in the trunk of their Lexus in the garage. It didn't take them long to be back in the Hollywood Hills. Noell began to tremble and her voice was near tears. "What's going to happen?" she asked awkwardly. "What am I about to find in our house?"

"Noell, look at me," Michael said in a soft voice. "Do you have a housekeeper?" When he received a little nod, he asked, "Is she scheduled for today?" Again he saw the nod. "Then you are going to find your home precisely as you left it. There is nothing to fear at all. I'm with you today." He held out his hand for her to hold in confirmation.

"But it will be empty," she whimpered.

"It has always been empty. It's a lovely big house. I've been in every room. Will you try to see it as that, a lovely home that you and your kids are going to fill with laughter and love?" He continued to hold her hand.

"I think the reality of the moment is sinking in," she whispered. "What will I say if someone asks about a funeral?" Once again her frame trembled.

"Tell them that a memorial service is being planned for a later date. Take a big breath. Now another. You are calm and we are in control. Will you say that with me? We are calm and we are in control. We are safe." Michael was not aware of the assurance he was bringing to the back seat as well.

It took him a couple hours to clean all the weapons from the bags. A broom closet in the utility room made a convenient storage place and he vowed to get a couple locks on it so no prying eyes might be tempted. Rose, the cook came to the cottage to inform him that dinner was ready if he would like to join the family. She asked if he would like wine or a cocktail before eating.

"Thank you for offering, he replied. "I have never acquired a taste for alcohol, but I am a sugar fiend. I love apple juice, pineapple or orange juice."

A few minutes later he pushed away from the table saying, "Rose that was a fabulous meal! Thank you."

He wasn't sure how far to take it with the rest of the folks seated, however. His attempts at table talk had been pretty futile. Finally he asked, "What do you do around here for fun?"

Caleb finally answered, "I have some electronic games and we watch some TV." The lad shrugged, "we don't do much."

"Stars and little fishes," Michael said roughly. "That's what my dad used to say when he didn't want to cuss. Stars and little fishes, we need to do something about that. Does anyone know how to play Chinese Checkers?" Heads shook. "Do you have any pets, you know, a kitty?" Once again heads shook.

Noell tried to explain. "You see, Hein…" Her face took on a panicked expression. "Fun has never been a priority in this house." She took a deep breath.

"Well I'm just the driver around here," Michael said with a grin. "But my opinion is that kids ought to have some fun. Caleb, if you were to learn to play a musical instrument, what would it be?"

"The young boy perked up and said, "probably a piano would be fun to play, or maybe drums."

"O.K. How about you Camilla?" He hoped he was asking the correct girl. "What instrument would you like to play?"

"I'm Celia," she giggled, "and I'd like to play the violin."

"Me too," the real Camilla answered, "or maybe the flute. I think that is real pretty."

Noell had relaxed during this brief exchange. She realized that Michael had them talking about a personal interest. He was demonstrating that they were in fact safe and in control.

Before Michael returned to the cottage, he asked Noell to wear one of the small lapel transmitters. He would keep an ear bud in to make sure they were all safe. As the mom was tucking the kids in, Michael overheard Camilla ask, "Mom, do you think we could really have a kitty?" He knew it was Camilla. She had a sharper pronunciation of her "T."

The next morning after breakfast, Michael produced a sack with several games. Chinese Checkers consumed at least an extra hour at the table. Noell finally had to remind them to go get dressed. After lunch it was a domino set that was a bit advanced for the twins, but they loved to use the tiles like blocks to build towers and stuff. He showed them how to make a line of standing tiles that would self destruct. On Monday Michael took the girls on a shopping trip. First they found some play clothes, white for Celia, and light purple for Camilla were their personal favorites. That would help in instant identification. Then to a pet shop where they selected two female Siamese kittens. They named them Alice and Amanda.

The police finally listed the case as open but inactive. They had traced the nine French paramilitary as Soldier of Fortune contractors. Heinrik Ferraris' death was listed as a natural cause, the exertion of his home defense. No other explanations were available and the case would remain under review. His body was cremated.

The first sign of conflict came when Noell had an appointment with their attorney. She was informed that in matters of death, extra hours of research were required . Their bill was $20,000.

Michael said to Mr. Knapp, "Sir, this death occurred eight days ago and you are contending that forty hours of attorney time has been given to it. I'd like to see an itemized report before Mrs. Ferraris accepts it."

J. Gordon Knapp was not accustomed to being questioned about billings. "This is a routine matter when there is the death of someone as prominent as Heinrik, with as many investments and holdings. I assure you it is quite routine."

"Perhaps, sir, none the less, I am requesting an itemized report." Michael maintained a light attitude.

But Mr. Knapp wasn't. His voice took on a brittleness as he said, "Who are you to question this? You have no authority here. This is none of your business." A vein in his temple turned red and he appeared to be in some discomfort.

"What's the matter Mr. Knapp? Hasn't your firm taken enough from this account? I'll wager there is not more than thirty minutes of attorney time in this bill and an hour of a secretary, if that. This looks like a lot of hot air to me."

"That's enough!" he nearly shouted. "I'll ask you to leave this office or I'll call security."

Noell, who had been silent up to this point, said "That would be a mistake on so many levels. Mr. Winter is only speaking for me. That's authority enough." Her voice was soft and controlled. "If you should call them you would also need to call an ambulance for them. He asked for an itemized report. Is that worth violence or getting all upset?"

The counselor tore up the bill saying angrily, "We'll send you an itemized bill and the request that you find new legal representation. We no longer welcome you here." Michael stood up saying, "Yup, that's like shooting the Golden Goose, but it does prove my point. You would have been fired anyway."

They sat in the car for a moment. Noell looked at him and said, "You just saved me enough that I can keep you for two months. How did you know to question him?"

"I'll bet Mr. Knapp has been getting some sort of kickback from someone else involved in this. Is there anyone else you can think of who might want to contest the will?"

Noell thought for a moment. "He has a brother here. But they haven't spoken in years and I'm sure Phillip was not even mentioned in the will."

"Well then," Michael offered another thought. "Maybe it has something to do with whoever is managing your assets. There is no way a death would account for forty hours, of attorney time, unless Heinrik's will was being modified or challenged. As long as we are out, shall we go see who else we can rattle?"

Jinnison Investments was prominently located in a downtown high-rise. They were greeted by Sheri Shangrow, the manager. "I am so sorry to hear of your husband's demise. He has been one of our finest accounts." That was spoken sweetly. "But most recently his investment choices have been high risk, which haven't done so well." That was said with an apologetic voice.

Noell said in an equally apologetic tone, "I'm just trying to get all these loose ends tied up. May I have an itemized report of Heinrik's first quarter and current activity? That would be so helpful to us."

The manager was gone only a couple minutes before bringing back a four page report. "This is what has transpired on his account this calendar year." A quick glance showed a negative loss of thirteen million! The curious thing is that the company's total assets showed only a modest gain during that time.

When they were back in the car, Michael suggested, "Just one more stop. I believe you said your accounts are with Sierra Federal Bank. Let's get a print out of all the activity from savings and checking. Then we should see what you have to work with. Do you have enough energy for it?"

"I can't say this has been a fun outing. But I am seeing how regimented you are and how efficient. Let's get this and then get home." She was trying to be extra perky.

The lights were on quite late in the cottage. He would have missed it except his dad's birthday is March fourth and there was a significant withdrawal from the savings account on that date, but the trade report didn't match. It was for February twenty first, a Sunday. What firm does business on Sunday? First thing in the morning, Michael made a call to the FBI Security Fraud Division in D.C. "Good morning Harry. I'm Michael Winter. It's been a few years since we worked together. Yeah I was in drug enforcement. I hope you can help me." He listened and then thanked him with a quick report.

"I'm doing personal security now for a prominent Hollywood family. Yesterday I ran into an irregularity that you might be able to look into. Yeah, I think you call it a diversion of assets. There is a Jinnison Investments that is handling the account. Their trading reports seem to be doctored; they predate the actual purchase date when they know there is going to be a sharp drop. With a false closing report they have a quantity of income that seems to be going somewhere other than the business. I'm wondering if this might be middle east bound. If so, Homeland might be interested. Is David Williams still the Inspector General of the Postal Service? If you can pass this along for the right person to look into it I would be very grateful. There are millions of dollars unaccounted for." He gave the contact information and account numbers of both the investment firm and the Knapp attorney that might be involved as well.

By lunch there had been three Chinese Checker games and Michael had read the first two from Kipling's Just So Stories. He even tried to make strange voices to enhance the characters.

After lunch they all watched the tender video, Fly Away Home, which brought quite a few tears. Noell's were from feeling a tender closeness with and between her children. That was refreshingly new and due solely to Michael.

He had spent a few minutes straightening the cottage before turning out the lights when he heard her soft voice in his ear bud. "Can you hear me?" she asked softly. "I don't know what I would do without you. You make every minute of my day enjoyable." There was a long pause before she said, "I feel like you are right here with me. Good night my precious friend."

He smiled because for just that moment, he felt like he was there beside her too.

For the two weeks before school started the house was busier than Noell could recall There were frequent road trips to the zoo, the aquarium, a Dude Ranch where they actual got to ride horses and pet goats. The girls had a Suzuki violin teacher on Monday and Wednesday ; Caleb's piano teacher was on Tuesdays and Thursdays. In between times were for games and stories, It was wonderful. And every night he heard a sweet good night that was becoming more personal.

That tranquility was shattered on the third afternoon they went to pick up the kids from school. They were told, "Their father picked them up about fifteen minutes ago. He had identification and we remembered him from last year." A chill rattled Noell; this couldn't be happening.

Before she could get back to the car her cell phone rang; the caller ID indicated it was Heinrik! "Hello darling," his voice sounded strange to her. "Yes, I picked up the children since I was in the neighborhood. I assure you they are safe and snug for the moment. The question is how will you get them back?"

"Who are you?" Noell demanded.

"Darling, it is Heinrik, of course. Oh, you didn't know that poor Phillip was in the house the night of that dreadful bloodshed. I'm surprised they mistook his body for mine. But you know it is strangely liberating. I'm not sure how my brother feels about that. But the point is, the children will be waiting for you at his La Canada place in the gulley. I do hope you can recall how to find it, and please bring your bodyguard with you. I think we have a score to settle. Just come by anytime this evening. Remember it's a school night and the children need their rest." His voice was so cheery it made her nauseous.

She turned panicked eyes toward Michael and told him the content of the terrible call. "He wants you to come along too. It sounded icy threatening."

Michael nodded. "That sort of explains the attorney's fees. He was providing a phony ID for one of them. But which one was in the house that night?" He was quiet as he formed a plan. "You say the house is about an hour north of here? Let's stop by the cottage so I can pick up some stuff and then we'll go get the kids." He stroked her shoulder reassuringly. "I'm sure I can manage this."

The sun was setting as he finished his second sweep around the area, making sure he stayed out of sight. He parked the car on a cul-de-sac about a quarter mile from the target and asked Noell to please remain with the car. She would only complicate things if he had to watch after her too. Before he got out of the car she held his face for a moment. She said, "Please be careful and help the kids." Then she kissed him as she had wanted to do for a month.

Carrying the bag of equipment was complicated as he moved through the brush of the steep hillside. He had to remind himself that stealth was more important than speed, right now. The house was lighted and he could hear loud music. Mentally he assessed the defense as careless. They would not hear his approach or first engagement.

The outside guard was on the porch smoking. He was watching the driveway, oblivious to the possibility that attack might be approaching from behind. Michael scraped his fingernail across the canvas bag making a sound just loud enough to draw attention. When the guard looked around the side of the house a dart struck him in the neck. It carried a synthetic spider venom that instantly paralyzed him. The effects would only last a minute or two, but that was ample time for the ice pick to do its lethal work. The dead body was carried to the fence and seated against it. A second guard, looking for his comrade, fell victim in the exact manner.

With only one car parked in front of the house, Michael assumed there were no more than six opponents. He silently opened the back door and waited in the dark kitchen. "Paul, do you want a beer?" the voice asked as footsteps approached. Michael stepped back into a dark shadow. The dart was accurate and the effects fatal. Now there were three max. He put the ice pick in its scabbard at his back and pulled out Danny's pet .22. "Hey Jan, what's taking so long?" Michael could see the shadow approach with a gun at the ready. The instant there was a clear shot, the small silenced pistol took out another. Now there were two, max. But he cautioned himself to be watchful. He was beginning to believe these were not trained or skilled guards, just tough guys from the street. Still he listened for any clue. There were children's voices upstairs. The girls were crying and a gruff voice was trying to quiet them. Silently Michael moved toward the sounds, his watchfulness on full alert. At the top of the stairs there was an open door to a bathroom. Michael slid into the darkness knowing that if he was planning an attack it would be from just such a place. It was empty and he was prepared.

Ten silent minutes past, finally the children were quiet even though the gruff voice was speaking in a hushed threatening way. Finally Michael took a soap dish and tossed it over the railing into the front room. There was a loud clatter as it hit the floor.

Immediately the voice from the children's room called out, "Jan what was that? Paul is everything O.K.?" Michael was certain those men would not answer but he was wary that there still might be one more unaccounted for. Then the children's door opened and he could hear the shuffling of feet, little feet They were being used as a human shield. He listened as they were passing the open door and he counted to three. As he stepped out of the shadow the back off Heinrik's head was less than five feet from him. The .22 hissed and Michael grabbed the collar of the collapsing form. He didn't want the children to be knocked down the stairs. Everything was still, until the girls started to cry again. Michael bent down and embraced the children, assuring them that they were safe and he was there to take them home.

He asked Caleb if there were more than five men in the house. The lad shook his head saying, "Just Uncle Phillip and his four friends."

Finally Michael called Noell. "Everyone is safe and eager to see you," he said softly. "Come and pick us up."

When the car stopped the driver door burst open and the mom raced to hold her children. She kissed them and wept and kissed them again. Michael was turning to go back in the house until she grabbed him and kissed him eagerly. "Thank you again," she said breathlessly and there was another kiss.

He said he needed to retrieve his bag and arrange things a bit before they left. In just a few minutes he was back with a big smile. "I really missed you guys," he said playfully, hoping to chase away the bad images they had seen. They had driven halfway home when the timer on the incendiary grenade went off. Napalm burst over the interior of the house and the five bodies that were in the front room. Perhaps identification could be made from dental records in the ashes, but probably not. The La Canada Fire Department had a dickens of a time containing the blaze to just that canyon instead of having it spread to the houses on the hill.

The family was enjoying a late snack, a dish of Rocky Road ice cream. Caleb looked at Michael for a long moment before he said, "I wasn't afraid because I knew you would find us. You promised you would keep us safe. Stars and little fishes, I don't think Uncle Phillip is a very nice man." Michael smiled broadly as he gave them each a hug and told them again how proud he was of them. He said that he still had some work to do and they had school tomorrow.

An hour later he heard her soft voice say, "Michael, can you hear me? I need you to hold me." There was a long silence then she said again, "Please come in and hold me. Please."

They had a one o'clock appointment with Mr. Knapp, the attorney. They wanted to go over the will and make sure there were no irregularities. A contrite man assured them everything was just as it always had been. A cursory reading demonstrated the truth of that.

Michael placed a billfold on the desk saying, "I'm a bit confused however, what this might have to do with you."

The attorney opened it to find a familiar forgery: it was Phillip's driver's license, but the name was Heinrik Ferraris. "Where did you get this?" he asked with a trembling voice.

Michael said softly, "More to the point, why did you have it made for him?" The question was based more on presumption than evidence, but it struck a nerve.

Mr. Knapp stammered and looked at Noell in confusion. "I didn't… I don't know what you are implying."

"Come on," Michael said a bit less patient, "There was a hit planned for Noell and maybe the kids as well. That was much too complex for Heinrik to arrange alone. I'm guessing that it was your doing. Did you set that up? For sure you knew about it and the death of Heinrik meant the end of the milk run for you. Phillip must have made an agreement with you. Was he in on the original hit? It must have been shocking to learn that all nine of them were dead."

The attorney's face was ashen and he was beginning to sweat. "I have no idea what you are implying. This meeting is over."

Michael was pouring a glass of water for him. "I think you had your eye on the two hundred million or so in the estate. The divorce was going to mean a division of assets. You stood to lose a lot." He offered it to the frightened man, who drank gladly as a distraction. He had not noticed the small veil of clear liquid Michael had poured into the glass before the water, nor had he noticed the latex gloves that Michael now took off and placed in his pocket. "You don't look very well Mr. Knapp. I think you need some assistance. He stepped to the door and called for the receptionist to contact an aid car. With the rush of concerned people into his office, Michael and Noell made a discreet exit. The ambulance would not arrive before Mr. Knapp's heart stopped.

The car was quiet on the way home, both of them replaying the events of yesterday and now today. Finally Noell said, "It seems like a jumbled mess, all the death and intrigue. You just seem to rise above it effortlessly. You are a hero, my hero. All the loose ends are tied up and I do believe I am completely safe now. It terrifies me to think you might leave me." She looked at his strong face and happy eyes. "Michael I adore you. I fantasize about you. I don't know what I would do without you. Will you marry me?"

He started to chuckle, then realized she wasn't joking. He said softly, "I have no plans to go anywhere else." Then trying to put some humor in it he added, "I have the whole rest of the Just So Stories to read and.."

"Quit it," she said sadly. "I don't think you realize what a remarkable difference you have brought into our lives. My kids are coming to life after being squashed for years. I feel alive and hopeful because of you. I'm the flower and you are the sunshine. I don't think it is sick; I think it is wonderful. I wake up in the morning eager to see your face and smell your breath. How more clearly can I say it? I need you. I want you." She paused before saying softly, "I love you." Her gray eyes held his.

"O.K. Noell", Michael answered softly, "let me honestly tell you that much of what you have just said I would echo right back.

I've never had a serious relationship, probably because I have been so mobile in my missions. For four years I was a street bum to wage war on drug dealers. This is the first time I've ever gone to bed without setting out a couple guns and a knife for self defense. It's the first time I have wanted to purchase office casual clothes. I feel gentle when I'm with you and that is deliciously new. I love your kids and," he hesitated before saying, "I love you too. I've killed for you, not once but as much as it takes to keep you safe. I've been afraid that you are way out of my league. You will probably get tired of paying for my services and I'll be on my way somewhere else." His expression was serious, maybe even a little sad.

Now her countenance brightened. "So tough guy, what are we going to do about it. I don't want to waste another day. Will you marry me, or what?"

"Do I have to sign a prenuptial agreement?" Now the playfulness was back.

"No you don't. What I've got, you get. But you do have to adopt my kids. I want no more Ferraris names."

For the rest of the drive home he tried to keep them talking about her. She was born in Minneapolis. Her parents divorced when she was in grade school. Mom remarried a beach bum who was a film editor from California. After three years they divorced and she remarried a paper salesman named Ed Frost, who fathered Richie and Paul. Dad married an artist from Florida. They seem pretty happy but it had been years since she had seen them. Her brothers were eager to be on their own. One is a school teacher; the other is a corpsman in the Navy. He is currently in Iraq. She got into drama in high school, did a couple fun plays in college. There were a couple interested guys until Hollywood invited her to be a small part in a couple romantic movies and Heinrik discovered her. If she had it to do over, she would have become a family counselor. "But," she concluded, "my kids are the light of my life. When the twins were born my tubes were tied. I thought three would be enough to devote a lifetime to raising them." That was probably more information than she intended to share.

After supper, when all three children could agree that they had practiced 30 minutes, the family watched Finding Nemo, even though the twins admitted that there were some scary parts.

In the quiet darkness Michael heard her gentle voice again. "Michael can you hear me? Please come in. I want you to hold me and tell me it will be all right. Please. I want to feel you next to me, not just a listener in the night. Please." Her soft voice was like a prayer, which he answered.

By the end of September a federal audit revealed gross irregularities in the Jinnison management. A class action lawsuit froze their assets to repay the twenty two accounts that had lost significant investments. Three middle east recipients were targeted as extremist cells.

During that time Michael and Noell were married by a Judge with Mrs. Scott and her assistant as witnesses. The adoptions and Caleb's ninth birthday were celebrated by a trip to Disneyland. Noell commented that the children had never received so much attention from a dad who would even ride the roller coaster with them. Michael responded, "I've never had this much fun with kids who call me 'daddy'." And then they were five.

Soon the talk about the future became serious. Michael heard her express displeasure with the size of this mansion, the sprawling size of the city, the gross population, the smog, the Santa Anna winds, and the lack of other children in the neighborhood until finally he asked her, "If you could choose a new place to live, where would it be?"

"You're going to think I'm very fussy," she answered with a smile. "I know what I don't want more than what I do want."

"At least it is a place to start," he said with a grin.

"Well there should be no snowy winters and no steaming hot summers, no hurricanes or tornadoes and no poisonous snakes or spiders. I'd like a city with good shopping and fine dining on occasion." She was still for a moment as she thought, then she added, "It should be near an international airport and have lots of flowers. But mainly it should be a place with great schools and plenty of children." She nodded her head as though punctuating the thought.

"Sweetness, I believe you have described the temperate west side of the Pacific northwest. Portland and Seattle are the only international airports I can recall there. Portland is called the Rose City. It would be surprising to see how much less property costs there too." Michael didn't want to mention that he was familiar with the area.

"Does it rain a lot there?" she asked with a half smile. Before he could answer she said, "I sort of like rain that cleans the air and feeds the flowers."

He nodded, "It rains more than here and less than Minneapolis."

"Then let's go up and see what sort of houses and schools they have" She was sold on the idea, especially if it meant leaving this house with all its bad memories.

"Maybe I could call a realtor and have him line up some places for us to see," Michael suggested. Their "must have" list was not as long as he expected. She really did want to move.

Brad Stoddard welcomed them to the Portland office of Remax Realty. "You've chosen a great day to see some fine homes. I heard you say that schools are a high priority for you, so I have selected five in your generous price range in the West Hills. Beaverton and Aloha are the top school districts, probably because they are the newest with outstanding campuses. Do you have any questions before we get started?"

The first house was in a lovely residential area of Beaverton. With five bedrooms and four baths it would meet their needs, but it lacked the spark of interest for either Noell or Michael.

The second house was much the same, perhaps a bit more attractive than the first. But when Caleb said that all the houses on the block looked the same, they found little interest again.

The third house was on a corner lot in Aloha. Noell smiled at the name saying it was a pleasant greeting. The five bedroom, four and a half bath house, while new construction, had the feel of an older home. Caleb was attracted to the alcove room with a grand piano. The realtor explained that this was a distress sale. The family had divorced and the assets were being divided. He tried to brighten the picture by driving by both an elementary school and a middle school just minutes from the location.

The fourth home was a northwest version of what they already had in California: a gated driveway and immense structure. Noell was not even interested enough to look inside.

The fifth house was in Hillsboro, a short distance further west from the city. It had five acres with white fences and a definite rural feel. When the realtor pointed out the barn and the possibility of having horses, there was some interest from the twins, but not enough to take a serious look. The nearest neighbor was more than a half mile away. They headed back to the office with the assurance that there were five more for them to see tomorrow.

Michael pointed to an oddity they were passing. He asked, "Brad, can you tell me what's going on with that? I noticed it as we were going out." A large commercial looking structure was wrapped with plastic, much of which had been tattered by the elements and waved in a light breeze.

"Oh that is a colossal mess," the realtor said sadly. Su Products was a South Korean company that was going to make watercraft here, both power and sailboats. They didn't do their homework. The two acre plot is surrounded by residential commercial zoning, but not industrial construction. When the county red tagged the project, it went into legal efforts to rezone, which never happened. The Koreans went bankrupt. It has looked like this for almost a year while they duked it out. Sadly the construction company that got this far on the project has been left holding the bag and it looks like they are going to bite it as well. The whole mess is in the hands of the bank." He pointed out several other places of interest all the way back to the office.

Noell and the girls wanted to go to the Willamette Mall across the street from the hotel. The boys had a couple games of chess, one of which Michael was willing to lose. It would lead to another match later. The kids enjoyed the hotel's heated pool and finally they all agreed that the dining room had something yummy for every palate. All the while Michael was playing with a very extreme idea.

Finally when they could talk, Michael asked her what she had thought about the houses. Noell admitted that she was spoiled by the excessiveness of the Hollywood Hills, but that was a problem that she could fix. "The houses were adequate," she finally replied. "I wasn't blown away by any of them. I do like this area though. It seems more open and clean." She waited for him to ask more, and when he didn't she said, "What's on your mind. You've been sort of quiet all afternoon."

He kissed her gently. "Am I so easy to read?" He kissed her again. "I recall you saying that you would devote your life to raising your children. How serious did you mean that?"

"I was very serious. My devotion must always embrace you first, but I can't think of anything else as important as being a great mom." Her smile was warm and charming.

"You know how some families immerse their kids in sports?" he asked. "All year long they just go from one season after another." She nodded and he continued, "Some others may choose religion or science or cars. Others even allow their kids to choose their own excesses. All afternoon I have been wondering how I can help mold Caleb and the twins in a wholesome way. That never happened for me, so I don't have a good pattern to follow. When I saw that abandoned construction project I had an idea. What would it be like if there was a small performance venue where kids could play in a band together, or have fiddler's fiestas. You know, a place where there are lots of kids and lots of music. Do you think it would be right to immerse them in something like that? You know the thrill of being on stage and hearing applause for your talent. I think every child would welcome that."

Noell responded softly, "I don't know whether to laugh or cry. Heinrik never had a thought for anyone but himself. Now you have every opportunity to think extravagant thoughts and you are focused on the children. Do you wonder why I love you so desperately?" Once again she kissed him, but not so gently.

Michael smiled appreciatively. "I take it then you like the idea. The more I think about it the richer the idea becomes. It may be an activity that can consume some of our attention too. We need more intel, more information. Things could happen quickly if we get the right mix of folks working on it. Let's ask Brad to stop at the site tomorrow so we can get a better idea."

In the morning when Michael expressed an interest to stop at the construction site, Brad made a phone call to the Washington Mutual office and was told someone could be there in twenty minutes with the gate key.

The children waited in the car as the site was revealed to be larger by far than Michael had first thought. There was a full basement, originally planned for boat construction. The ground floor had a ridiculously high ceiling, at least thirty feet or more. Apparently it was meant to be a display room. There was a full floor above that, probably intended for sales and office spaces. After a few minutes, Michael thanked the Washington Mutual officer and offered his contact information. "I am interested in a cash buy out. Let me be clear. I don't bargain like an auctioneer. You send me your numbers and I will respond. There will not be an additional offer. We may work out conditions of the sale. I appreciate your courtesy this morning."

The first two homes Brad showed them were much like yesterday's, attractive but without unique appeal. The next two were estates on large acreage. Once again she shook her head. The fifth one was a modern beauty on a steep slope. It had plenty of space and an outrageous view. Noell smiled and said "no thank you" to the prospects of rescuing the children from the sheer sloping terrain if they ever fell off the porch.

Brad was feeling a little frustrated until Michael asked if they could see the corner lot one from yesterday. That had sort of grown on them. The family walked through the house twice, chatting about possibilities. It did have five bedrooms plus an office, a large formal dining room and great room. For Caleb, that piano in the alcove was a clincher.

Michael took out his checkbook and wrote an earnest payment check, offering 90% of the asking price and including the furnishings.

Sunday morning as the family returned from breakfast, they found a young man waiting by their door. He introduced himself, "I'm Kenny Fox, owner of Multnomah Construction. I'd sure appreciate a bit of your time to talk about the Su project."

The kids went into the big bedroom to watch cartoons. A serious conversation was begun around the table. Kenny said, "Brad is a personal friend. He called me about your interest in the debacle. I'm so grateful that there is a ray of hope. You may be all that's standing between me and bankruptcy, which for a contractor is a kiss of death." He took a breath and began, "The Su folks paid cash for the property. That became their equity against the loan." He offered them a sheet of paper. "That was $200K, Permits and design was $140K, Site work and drainage was$ 65K, Utilities was $45K, reinforced concrete foundation and basement was big, $290K, Steel framework was $287K, 2x6 roof and sides was $139K, the Steel roof was $195K, 24 double pane windows were $20K, and the six picture windows in the front were 30K. He caught his breath. "There are several incidentals trying to make it secure, but this gives you the big picture."

"Now the rub comes in," the young man continued, "when Su couldn't get the zoning changed and went belly up. The bank quit paying my bills after the utilities. In other words, they are $50K in unsecured debt and holding the purse strings. I'm in for a million unsecured." He shook his head. "I'm not sure what I can ask from you. I guess I want you to know where the money has gone and how the bank is going to try to turn this into a money-maker for them. If I'm going down, I hope you will let them go down too." His face was strained.

Michael reached over and gave Kenny's neck a bit of a rub. "Tell you what," he said with a chuckle, "let's not think about the sinking ship for a little bit. What we got excited about is the possibility of turning this into a small music venue, an auditorium with a simple stage where kids can make music. Do you think that could happen?"

Kenny shrugged, "Yeah, right now it's just a big box. I suppose we could fill it any way you'd want."

Michael asked, "Do you have an engineer or architect that could design those changes?" Before he could answer, Michael was sliding his contact information to him. "Just give me a call and I'll take care of the costs, and hopefully by the end of the week we can do something about this stuff too."

"Oh Lord," Kenny sighed, "My wife Cheryl is expecting our first child and this has been hanging over our heads for months. You may be our God-send."

Michael took three twenties out of his wallet. "Until then, why don't you take her out to dinner tonight and tell her the cavalry is right over the hill. I like the stuff you showed us today. You and I are going to work together just fine.

Noell and Michael talked about the possibilities of this project at length. She was concerned about the cost until he reminded her that the sale of the Hollywood Hills home would pay for this four or five times over. Finally the family walked to the new Cinema Theater where they ordered grilled ham and cheese sandwiches, fries and a milk shakes from their reclining upholstered seats. The new movie WALL-E delighted them all.

At precisely 10:00 a.m. Michael asked the Washington Mutual receptionist if he could speak to the Commercial Construction Manager.

Politely she asked, "Do you have an appointment?"

Michael displayed his FBI badge and ID replica. In a less than friendly voice he growled, "No, lady, I don't need one. I'm Michael Winter from Federal Reserve Compliance Division, here to schedule a bank wide audit and training program."

The young woman rose immediately to report that a very grouchy man with a badge wanted to speak with Mr. Greg Peterson.

A well dressed middle age man offered Michael his hand, saying "Good morning, I'm Greg Peterson, Construction Manager. What can I do for you, sir?" He was not the same man who had brought the site key on Saturday.

Michael ignored the handshake and said simply, "Well Mr. Peter, you could begin by reading the Consumer Protection Act bulletin that has been circulated by the Federal Reserve. Out here in the sticks you may not feel a need for compliance. The president has not yet signed the Dodd-Frank Act into law, but will soon. Chapter three of that act would have been of significant interest to you. Janet Yellen, the Fed Chair, has received a complaint that would have been easily avoided if you had only been up to speed on compliance." He scowled as though quite angry. "Mr. Peter, ..."

"It's Peterson," the gentleman corrected.

"Mr. Peter, your bank has been named in a complaint that is about to cause a lot of folks a lot of grief. If you had read the bulletin you would have known it is your responsibility to protect subs and suppliers when a loan goes into default. You should have stopped work on the Su Products construction immediately, as soon as the bankruptcy was announced. Instead you allowed the Multnomah Construction to accrue a million dollars in unsecured debt. Damn it, that's just wrong. Did you think he could read your mind? Now I have to shut you down for an annual audit and compliance training. By the time our auditors are finished with you a trip to your proctologist will seem like a Sunday stroll. Are there any other Wa Mut branches?"

"Washington Mutual" he clearly pronounced the name, "has thirty two branches in Oregon and Washington." The man said proudly.

"Oh for Christ' sake!" Michael exploded, "That will take all of our auditors and trainers at least a month to get to all of those!" Michael softened his voice and added, "He tried to tell you that there is new money on the table. He had an easy solution for you Mr. Peter, but I guess your way is old school ignorance." He shook his head in disbelief. "Block off all of next week for the first of the audits and branch-wide training. The banks will be closed in seriatim. We'll contact the others. I'll bet your name becomes a dirty word." Michael stood as though to go.

"Wait, Mr. Winter," the now focused banker understood the gravity of the moment. "I haven't heard of any options. What can I do to expedite a solution here?" It was obvious that Mr. Peterson was alarmed.

"Listen, Mr. Peter, I'm in compliance not mortgage. It seems to me that you should be talking to the contractor that you hung out to dry. I believe you are squatting on the key and have been all along. You have the title to the property as the only viable asset. Send it to Columbia Title, along with all your expenditures. They will repay you and the contractor as well. Then the project can move along. It seems awfully easy to me, but then I'm in a different discipline. I'll wait until Wednesday morning before ordering the audits and training." Without any courtesy handshake, Michael walked out of the office. He was pretty sure it would all work out now.

By noon he had outlined his plan with Kenny. "I'll be home in time to wire $1M to you and $250K to Columbia Title in care of you. Just make sure we get that title free and clear before the bank gets theirs. I'll be eager to see some concept drawings when they are available. Do you feel better now, dad?" He listened to joyful relief.

Kenny said, "This is amazing! I was certain my building days were over. But I don't know what you get out of this deal."

"Think about it," Michael said confidentially. "I'm paying the amount owed on all the construction activity to date. For my effort I get the title to the property free and clear. That's what the Su folks lost and I gained. Pretty good for a weekend's work, huh?"

His final call before they went to the airport was to Brad at Remax. "Hey Brad, you folks receive a listing fee don't you?" He listened then replied, "Well brother, we have a monster place that we want to list soon, like as quickly as I can have it appraised. Then I'll know an asking price. If the past is any indicator, we'll have it sold within the month." He listened for a moment, then answered, "Of course you can come down. We have a guest cottage with three bedrooms. If you can do the job I'll be happy to see you receive the commission. Now tell me about our offer for the Aloha place." He listened again. "Yes, I'm sorry for them. Set up a signing date for us and they'll get wired right back to you. Thanks to you we have a vested interest in an abandoned project that may see new life as well. Yeah I think so. You might get fresh information from Kenny Fox. I'm really glad you called him."

In the darkness of their cozy bed, Noell snuggled tight against Michael and said, "You are a constant surprise to me. When you said you would wire the money for our new project I didn't know you meant from your private account. Is there a reason you didn't use ours?" He felt her try to get even closer to him.

"Noell, I look back at the past twelve or thirteen years and wonder who that man was. I did things I will never tell you about. As we waged war against drug lords, we confiscated a lot of money. Can you imagine a field pack with fifty pounds of $100 bills and a duffle bag with three times that? It was either take it with us or blow it all to hell. I have seven accounts that I consider my retirement. Today I used a part of one of those. I believe I am cleansing the money by a noble use of it."

Her soft voice asked, "Then you're not going to dump me for a more exciting project?"

In just a few moments they demonstrated the true meaning of exciting project.

Mr. Peterson tried one small push-back on the proposal. But when he was told that the property title was not an inflatable asset in the financial equation, and Washington Mutual could eat the unsecured $50K loss and plan for an immediate audit and compliance training, the logical conclusion was reached and they signed off on everything. Just as Michael had prayed.

Alpha Design listened to Michael's idea for a music venue and created plans for an auditorium with 700 seats, counting the balcony. A second request was the design for the second floor. Utilizing two standard elevators and a freight elevator, the basement could become covered parking. Noell wondered if they could utilize the top floor space as a residence, with four or five bedrooms, four and a half baths, plus two guest suites and lots of open space. There was even ample room for a generous commercial food court as well as their residence. The territorial views allowed both morning and afternoon sun.

The Jinnison funds were finally released and turned into interest bearing federal bonds. The Hollywood Hills mansion was sold in a bidding war. The final bid was 10% over the asking price because they wanted the furnishings, especially the paintings. Finally, Mayflower packed and moved their personal things to the Aloha house. There was still time to decorate for Christmas.

Noell tried not to concern herself overly with bad omens, but she couldn't get it out of her mind that the downtown Pioneer Christian Church burned to the ground on Christmas Eve. She wondered what other calamities might be lurking.

Not many folks had Michael's cell phone number, so when it rang he was immediately curious. "Hey Chief," the voice was familiar and strangely welcome. "Are you busy for a few days?"

"Randall, it's good to hear your voice, you old dog. I thought your hide would be tacked up on a barn somewhere by now." They both chuckled.

"I miss you too, Mike. But this is not a social call. Colonel Paris Sherman has moved over into NSA and is trying to regroup the old strike team. He is in charge of information extradition. When folks take our secrets, he gets them back. Denny and I need your help, Bro. Have you got a few days to go to Dubai?"

"You say Sherman is a full Colonel?" Michael asked trying to give himself a few moments of consideration.

"Yeah, we all get next rating. If you will join us you'll get back pay to your separation date as a WO4. The target is a woman who was at the Patent Office. She copied a load of important innovations that could hurt us if it goes public, from military weapons, to pharmaceuticals, to new technology. The Chinese would love to get their hands on it."

There was a long pause before Michael asked, "Wouldn't it be SOP (standard operating procedure) to send in a team of Feds to bring her home?"

"Right." Randall agreed, "But we don't have a treaty with the Emirates, so we need to improvise." He could tell that Michael wanted to turn down the operation. "Our intel is that she is squirreled up in a luxury hotel with some bodyguards and has invited a lot of bidders into her yard sale. It should be an easy in, easy out. Four days max." Before Michael could reply, Randall added, "There is an F-18 waiting for you at the 23rd Air Base at Portland International."

To say that Noell was unsupportive of the idea would be an understatement. She was mortified at first and then terrified that he might be in harm's way and not return. Michael assured her that Kenny would check in with her each day. "I'll be home by Sunday afternoon." There wasn't much she could do about it but weep.

The operation began by turning off the power to the second floor, which opened all the solenoid locked doors. The first guard that tried to prevent them from entering was hit with a dart, the other two fell to Denny's .22. Three hours later a naked woman, who had been heavily sedated, was trying to explain why she had no memory of the deaths of those three men. Her chemically induced amnesia did not appear to be temporary. Without luggage, money, I.D, or most importantly, computer related items, she could not give them her name, nationality nor her purpose for being in Dubai. Her room, including the safe, had been stripped of all contents.

On the flight home Michael shared with them his new life in Portland. Both of his buddies could understand his reluctance in being gone from home. They both agreed, however, that the mission had been a total success and were sure Col. Sherman would be pleased with their report.

If his departure had been sad, his homecoming was immeasurably happier! Noell's greeting was tender and her embrace made it clear that she meant every word of it. She admitted that the four days had been busy. "Kenny and Cheryl brought us supper one night and invited us to their home for lunch yesterday," she reported, still holding him tightly. "They are so very grateful that the project is back underway. Her due date is just around the corner. It could be a New Year baby."

Enjoying her soft warmth, Michael whispered, "I think '09 is going to be terrific!"

"Daddy, may I ask you a question?" Camilla's soft voice got his attention.

"That is a question Sweetie. What else would you like to ask?" It was a rare moment when one of the twins would instigate a conversation.

"We like Mrs. Fisk a lot." She paused trying to think how to say a hard thing. "She's been a good teacher and we know you like her too. But..." She couldn't bring herself to voice a harsh judgment.

"Cam, sweetie, are you having trouble with her lessons? Is she going too fast for you girls?" If she couldn't voice it, perhaps he could stumble along for them.

"Oh, stars and little fishes!" the surprising outburst made Michael smile. "She's not too fast. It's just the opposite. She's had us in the beginning book for three and a half months. Cele and I had that finished in a week. She wants us to play slow. Listen." She picked up her violin and played a familiar tune, as Cele joined them.

"I have heard you play that, and you do it well."

"But Daddy, listen how it sounds if I play the notes as quarter instead of whole." Suddenly her violin was happy and alive. He tapped his toe to the improved version. "Doesn't that sound righter to you?" she asked.

Cele lifted her violin and played the same happy tune again with her sister. Cam said, "We've found out that every tune has a twin in it." This time Cele played the tune briskly and Cam played the same rhythm but new harmonizing notes.

"That's beautiful," Michael said in wonder. "Where did you learn that?" His smile was broad and assuring.

"We didn't learn it, daddy," Cele answered. "That's just the twin song. They are real playful. We love playing together."

Cam said a bit softer, "Cele likes to make it dance, and I like to make it sing the twin song."

"Sweetheart," the amazed dad said, "that's called harmony. That's what makes music reach our soul."

Michael called Mrs. Fisk, who was not surprised that the girls wanted a more challenging teacher. "They deserve one," was her only response. She gave him the name of the first chair at the Portland Symphony, who immediately declined any teaching role. She did, however suggest that Michael contact Lester Klein, second chair. He frequently took on promising students.

Mr. Klein was less than enthusiastic about twin six year old students. They were a bit older than the devoted ones he had worked with in the past. But when Michael let slip the concept of a music venue for youth activities, Mr. Klein was completely engaged. He said he never did home-visitation teaching. But when Michael mentioned that he would need to find someone who could organize a youth symphony. Lester made an appointment to come to Aloha and meet the girls. It was to be the destined elements of wonder. For the rest of the winter he met with Cele and Cam twice a week. He remarked that their phenomenal musical acquisition was electric. They were already well advanced.

Michael had another request from Col. Sherman in February. He was gone for five days. A Second Lieutenant had assaulted a junior officer. When she brought charges against him, instead of facing a court marshal he fled to Vietnam, where there is no extradition treaty. The trio caught up with him at a seaside resort, where an unexplained riot started and the fugitive was fatally injured. Once again Col. Sherman would give high marks for the plan and execution of it.

This trip home had an unusual ending however, because they talked about what they would like to do with the rest of their lives. It began when Michael described the Harmony House and their plans for it. Randall wistfully admitted that he had always imagined how much fun a dance studio would be. Denny shared that customizing cars had been a passion in high school. Now it could be a dream come true. Just before they landed at Travis, Michael explained that a righteous use of the confiscated funds had given him a sense of peace. His partners nodded, admitting that was something they still wrestled with. "You will never know how terrific it can be unless you try," he said. His thoughts were about holding Noell.

The auditorium was pretty well finished by Easter. The twins seventh birthday was just three days later. It wasn't a planned celebration, but when KGW channel 4 requested a walk-through to introduce the new "Harmony House," a name chosen by the children, it became one. Noell agreed to be the spokesperson, if the twins could play their violins as representatives of future activities.

The camera followed the movements of two little girls who seemed to play for one another and the music was mesmerizing.

Finally, Noell assured Pam Lewis, the interviewer, that the structure was to be non-commercial. "We envision this building to be a place for children to find their voice and talent," Noell said softly to the camera. "We are non-profit. Our goal for this year is to collect instrument donations, which we will make available to any school student in the hopes of starting a ground-swell of young music makers. We have envisioned some fall galas, but have nothing on the calendar at this time. It has been important to complete the auditorium first. We've been contacted by the Tuba Christmas folks who will be on stage at least one night, maybe two. The project is just ready to receive requests. By this time next year we hope there will be the beginning of an Aloha Youth Symphony."

"That does sound energetic," Ms. Lewis said with a charming smile. "Will there be some fund-raising opportunities for folks, or a way to make donations.

Noell said sweetly, "I'm sorry if I failed to mention that this is non-profit; we will not encourage outside assistance. A generous philanthropist has guaranteed us ten years of support. That should be time enough to tell if this is a worthy endeavor."

Ms. Lewis tried once more to peek into the organizational structure. "Then is Harmony House connected to some faith-based organization or political group?"

Noell's expression remained pleasant but her tone of voice took on a less cheery tone. "Pam, I'm not sure why you would ask me that. I thought I made it clear that this non-profit effort is solely for children. Harmony House has no other purpose or connection than music. I suppose in your business you must try to turn over rocks and look for less gracious things. That's what makes your ratings I suppose. That's just sad." She took off her microphone before the startled news person could respond. The interview was over and that last part would be deleted, but the area wide listeners who had an interest in music, had seen and heard two amazing violinists.

That interview, combined with the two articles Michael placed in the Oregonian and Times, brought results. At first it was a smattering of donated instruments. Violins seemed to be the most common, but there were a few guitars and flutes. Then requests for beginner lessons became routine for every day. By the summer break, Lester Klein had recruited four teachers and distributed three dozen refurbished instruments. Tuesday and Thursday afternoons became a common drop-in practice time for any student to play with their peers. It was noisy and quite fun for them to realize it was a learning time for all. Noell had wanted children to play with hers. Boy, did she get them!

Noell pulled Michael's arm around her and spooned against him in the darkness. She pressed against his body in a way that she knew gave him pleasure. "Thank you again for today," she said softly. "When you told Caleb that the grand piano was being delivered to the stage, he felt very honored that you would ask him to come along." She moved ever so slowly. "He told me that you said it was for him, if he wants to be a leader in the youth symphony." She moved again, a bit more playfully. "He also told me that he had almost forgotten about the house and trouble in California. I love what you have done for us." She had moved enough to make her point. She giggled in pleasure.

By September Mr. Klein had organized three classes of violins. The third class were beginners. Second class intermediates and first class, which included the twins, was ready for performance. Eleven teachers were delighted to have the students and support in such an inspiring opportunity. It was time to display their talent.

Pam Lewis from KGW contacted Noell for another interview. "Noell, I am so sorry that our first coverage was so misunderstood. I truly apologize for my cynicism. I've been at this business long enough to forget that there are still some wonderful people. You are one of those for giving me a second chance. When my daughter Polly asked me if she could have lessons I was sure that I had been right.

I waited for some revelation of expenses. But then she was given a darling instrument and the only charges were for each lesson she had at Mrs. Crenshaw's home. When I see the scope of this I know it is a truly wonderful blessing for our region." She had a marvelous story that announced the introduction of "Fancy Fiddles". It would be an evening of children and members of the Portland Symphony having a memorable time together. Seating was limited to the first 700.

The evening began with a young trio, Caleb Winter and his twin sisters Celia and Camilla playing Debussy's *Clare de Lune.* There were several in the audient who felt that pleasant prelude was the best part of the evening. When it seemed that most of the seats were full, Mr. Klein welcomed the folks to the remarkable first performance in Harmony House. He thanked the folks who had the vision to make this possible and then introduced Kim Nguyen, first chair and concert master of the Portland Symphony. She raised her violin and played *Paganini's Capriccio in G minor* as a beautiful reminder of how passionate the violin can be. Then she played a stately rendition of *"America the Beautiful"*. Mr. Klein then introduced six more members of the string section of the symphony and he joined them as they played a much more moving rendition of it. Class three was introduced. First the children played their song and then the eight professionals joined them, playing simply but beautifully. Class two had a gentle version of *"Battle Hymn of the Republic"*, first played by the children and then the whole group. Class one played *"God Bless America* with more skill and feeling than folks expected. When the symphony folks joined them the audience stood and then clapped vigorously. It was not a lengthy program but for the parents it was a profound one. There was the promise of much more to follow.

In the milling moments after the program, Michael and Noell were standing with Kenny and Beth Fox, chatting about the wonderful venue and evening. An elderly woman, dressed in black, approached politely waiting for Noell's attention. She asked if she was the fortunate mother of the young pianist and adorable twins.

Noell was struck by her white hair, blue eyes, a host of wrinkles and quiet dignity.

"Yes, I am delighted to be their mother," she answered happily.

"As well you ought to be," the woman replied. "I'm Elva Gleason. I was blessed with a twin named Erma, and know well the joy of a loving mother. Please forgive my boldness. I have a gift I would like to bring to the children at your convenience." Her clear blue eyes held Noell's.

"That is very thoughtful of you," the mom said. "May I ask the nature of the gift?" She had no desire to become caught up in some sales scheme.

"Yes dear," she answered with a smile. "I understand the caution you have after such a trying time in California."

A shiver of anxiety gripped Noell. How could anyone know about their former challenges? For goodness sake, they had even changed their names.

Before she could reply, the elderly woman went on. "Forgive me for being so casual about that. I simply mean it is wise to be cautious." She took a deep breath and stepped a bit closer to Noell. "I have two very special violins I would like to donate," she said softly. "They are quite old but perfect for the twins. One is white and the other lavender. I noticed that the girls wore just those colors this evening." Her smile faded a bit. "The only stipulation I ask in this donation is that the violins must always be together. That's how we received them when we were the same age as your lovely girls."

Noell was a bit puzzled so she replied, "If they are so valuable perhaps you should keep them. You know the children are not always careful in their learning."

Now the wistful smile returned. "As I said, the violins must not be separated. When Erma finished her life, I knew I could not play mine again. I believe you will come to realize, as we did, that the violins are quite priceless....together. I can only give them to talented twins, which I have just found your darling daughters to be."

It sounded a bit bazaar, sort of like knowing that they had trouble in California, but finally Noell gave her their address and agreed that any time Monday would be a fine time to stop by."

Noell suggested that they go out for supper as a way of celebrating the successful day. She suggested Anthony's for fine dining. The family vote was four to one in favor of Appleby's for burgers. She assured them that a burger could, under happy conditions like this, be called fine dining too. They had just placed their order when Michael's cell phone buzzed him. He and Noell exchanged a long look. They were pretty sure it was not a local call. Yup, it was Randall.

"Sorry to rain on your parade Bro, but we've got a problem." Michael could tell this was serious for there was none of the usual bantering before getting to the main course. "A Corporal at Fort Leavenworth hit the arsenal this morning, with an accomplice. They killed three guards and loaded four rocket launchers and two dozen rockets. The accomplice was hit with a couple rounds during the scuffle. He lived long enough to tell us that the blue moving truck is headed for Canada. The plan is to load it on a Vancouver freighter bound for the Persian Gulf. Here's the rub. He's already got a twelve to fourteen hour jump on us. We're in Virginia and even with a jet, we couldn't catch up. He could be in your neck of the woods as we speak. We have alerted the Highway Patrol. But this isn't a sure thing or high on their priorities. Sherman wants this guy stopped cold. He doesn't want this to be a plea bargain or lengthy trial deal. If you can catch up with him it should go down without prejudice or consideration. He killed three of ours."

Michael finally had time to ask, "How will I identify the truck?"

"It's a blue International Box Truck with a Nebraska license and 'Mountain Movers' on the side doors. At night he could pretty easily slip across the border with a phony bill of lading. I hope you can prevent that from happening."

Michael asked the serving person if they could get their order to go. "An emergency has just come up."

He drove his family home and was in the garage lock-box just long enough to get some armament. Then he promised to be back by "this time tomorrow."

He drove north on I-5, going faster than trucks but aware that a weary driver might need a rest area. To make sure he didn't pass the blue truck Michael took a quick sweep through every rest area he came to, the one north of Vancouver, the one just past Kelso, the one near Olympia, the one south of Seattle. He wondered if this could possibly work. He drove slowly through the rest area north of Smokey Point and the one south of Bellingham. It was about midnight, that's when he saw it, parked over to the side with its lights off. He called Randall to report that he had the target in his sight.

"Take him down, man. Do not let that truck make it to Canada!" Randall's voice was strong and convincing.

Michael made sure there was no one around to witness, then he knocked softly on the truck door. Speaking in a slurred voice like one who had too much to drink he asked, "Hey man, can you give me a ride home?" He knocked a little louder and heard a sleepy voice "Beat it bum. I got nothing for you."

Michael knocked again, a bit louder. He was pretty sure that would do it. The driver side window slid down a bit and a growling voice said. "Get the hell off my truck. The only thing you're going to get here is hurt!" He probably didn't hear the .22 that hit him in the throat that also took out his spinal cord and certainly not the one an instant later when he was hit in the temple by a kill-shot. Wearing latex gloves, Michael reached in to unlock the door so he could roll up the window and relock the door. It would be a puzzle to whomever discovered him.

Back in his car, Michael called Randall to report a successful intervention and where authorities could catch up with the truck. Before he finished the call he said, "Tell Sheridan I am no longer accepting assignments. This one was too far over the line. I am not his personal assassin. I've never felt as dirty as I do right now. Cross my name off the list." He ended the call without saying farewell.

It was still dark when he crawled into bed beside a sleeping Noell. He told her that he loved her too much to ever leave her again. He said he would just grab a nap.

The doorbell awakened Michael a little after nine o'clock. Quickly he dressed and ran a brush over his short hair. He could at least look awake.

The family was admiring two shiny violin cases. They appeared to be brand new and yet quite old at the same time.

"Oh good morning Papa," the elderly lady said with a happy voice. "In your eyes I can see my own dear father's. He too served the king as a strong arm of justice." Michael didn't know what to do with information that was too personal for a first meeting. "I was just telling Celia that my name means 'elf' as does hers. I'll bet she is the busy prankster in this home. I delight in her spirit." Then looking at Camilla she said more softly, "And you are the blessed defender. I can feel Erma's presence in your spirit. You must be the thinker, the moderator, the peacemaker." Her voice broke with emotion. "Oh, how I miss my Erma," she murmured.

Trembling a bit, she shook her head as though regaining control. "Let me quickly tell you the secret of these instruments." Opening a case she reveled a shiny white violin. "This one was mine. I was chosen for it when I was just six." Affectionately she lifted the treasure and held it to her chin. With hands painfully twisted by age, she played just nine ascending notes. Looking intently at Cele, she asked, "Do you hear the dance? It is lifting its voice." She played them again. "Will you remember that small melody?" Cele thought it was a simple test, so she nodded. She could remember that. "You will want to change the dance, but it is very important that you do not." The woman gently handed the violin to its new mistress.

Opening the second case she revealed an instrument that seemed to change colors from lavender to pink to rich purple. "This was Erma's and she loved it with all her heart." She seemed to have difficulty lifting the violin to her chin. When she stroked the bow across the strings her gnarled fingers again played nine notes, four descending, one repeated and four ascending. Cam smiled for she immediately understood that her final note would be a fifth lower than Cele's, a perfect twin song apart. "Do you hear the song?" the woman asked, already sure of the answer. She played it again. "Will you remember that?" she asked on the verge of desperation. As Cam nodded, the woman said, "You always did remember it, dear. How I treasure your dependability." Reverently the violin was passed to the next generation.

She had accomplished her task, so Elva rose and started toward the door. "Remember," she said in parting, "whether you are in concert, playing for a wedding or funeral, visiting the jail or hospital, let them sing their melody at least once together. The effect will be amazing to you. Then you will understand."

Michael offered the mysterious woman a printed card, saying, "Here's a form to claim your donation as a tax deduction. Thank you for your gracious gift."

Her smile was fragile as she answered, "That won't be necessary, but your vigilance will be, Papa. You must guard the girls, for there are many who will try to take advantage of their gift." Her blue eyes held his and in that instant he knew that her words were true. As abruptly as she had arrived, she departed.

At first the girls simply admired the instruments, until Cele lifted hers out of the case. "It's bigger than my violin, but lighter, and look how long the bow is!"

Cam gently allowed her fingers to caress the beautiful violin, still resting in its case. "It seems too wonderful to be mine. May I play it?" she asked no one in particular.

Cele stroked the bow across the strings, making a rich soft sound. Then her fingers moved and she began playing their simple scales. A contented smile dawned on her face. "It is so beautiful," she said softly. For more than an hour the twins became familiar with their wonderful violins, and the instruments became familiar with their wonderful new owners.

One morning at breakfast, Michael asked Caleb, "Buddy, you have a major birthday coming soon. Where would you like to go for your celebration? Last year we went to Disneyland. Can you think of some place that would be fun?" His warm smile suggested to Caleb that his dad wanted to have some fun too.

"Do we have to go some place?" the lad asked. "I can't think of anyplace I like more than here." He thought for a moment then added, "Cele and Cam got to play their violins on TV for their birthday. Do you think we could have a piano party at Harmony House?" It was an idea that had little preparation time.

"When you think about it, what do you imagine that would look like?" Michael was thinking that two weeks was not a lot of time, but on the other hand, look what had already been accomplished. They simply needed a good idea and lots of helping hands.

"Mr. Lamb has three other students here" Caleb quietly offered. "Maybe we could have him play first, like the symphony violins, and then we could play our favorite song." Caleb's grin erased any doubt that this was his idea of a great party.

Justin Lamb, the piano teacher, lived at home while he was finishing his graduate work at Portland State University. He was doubtful that any sort of program could happen in just two weeks, until he heard the generous offer of an honorarium and the announcement that KGW would have a camera crew there. After all, the students had been working diligently on some special music. Why not show that off? And yes, he could provide a few minutes explaining the adaptability of the piano to different aspects of music appreciation. His only requirement would be an additional grand piano at Harmony House. Michael smiled knowing that would be the easiest part of the equation.

The auditorium was not quite full but nearly. In addition to the families of the four students, there were many of Mr. Justin's friends and professors from school, plus a good number of future students and teachers of Harmony House. There were even folks who were just curious to hear music played in a marvelous free venue.

Carrey James, the oldest of the four students, played Handel's triumphant march from Judas Maccabeus. Folks from the church would recognize the tune as *"Thine Be the Glory."* It was a super way to begin a recital.

Justin Lamb introduced himself and took his place at the other grand piano. He explained a bit of the history of the piano from harpsichord to modern electronic synthesizers. "It may have the sound of inspiration," he played a verse of the hymn *"Holy, Holy, Holy."* "It may have the melody of the patriotic," he said playfully as he gave a rendition of *"Yankee Doodle."* He continued, "It can be carefree," as he burst out a short bit of *"Honky-tonk."* "Or it can be thoughtful and timeless." He slid into Beethoven's *Sonata #23 in F minor, called the Appassionato.* He concluded, "Depending on the time, place, intent and ability of the musician, the piano is a delightful instrument." It was time to hear from his students.

"Jeff James, Carrey's brother, is our youngest student. He is seven years old and has been studying the piano for three years." He played Beethoven's *Fur Elise* with more skill and feeling than most folks expected from a young student.

"Jon Martin is a three year student as well. He is eight years old, playing, *"Jesu Joy of Man's Desiring"* by J. S. Bach." The familiar hymn tune was recognized and appreciated.

"Caleb Winter is a two year student who is ten years old. He has selected Pachelbel *Canon in D,* a challenging classic." Caleb began gently and allowed the Canon to build impressively. There was considerable applause for his talent.

"Our final solo student is Carrey James, who presented our prelude. She is also ten years old having five years of training. She has selected *Beethoven's Sonata # 14 in C sharp minor.* You will recognize it as the beautiful *Moonlight Sonata."* The auditorium was still and charmed by her skill.

The applause lasted until a smiling Mr. Lamb stood and thanked the folks. "We have one last attempt that we have only rehearses a few times. It is our eight hand tribute to America." Both pianos had two players seated on the benches. There were also brave parents seated around the room who began singing the words as the pianos played, "*My country, 'tis of thee,* sweet land of liberty, of thee I sing…" The words were printed in the recital folder. Each verse was played a bit better and louder as a wave of patriotism filled the large room. They all sang to the conclusion.

"Thank you again for your support and interest in Harmony House" Mr. Lamb fairly beamed. "My concluding task tonight is to tell you that this was a birthday wish. Caleb was asked where he would like to go for his birthday and without hesitation he asked to be here tonight with you all. His sisters will lead us as we sing our best wishes to him." Cele and Cam stepped into the light, one wearing a white dress and the other a lavender one, just a match to their violins. Their broad smiles hid the nervous jitters they felt until their first bow strokes. They played a simple phrase, nine notes in harmony, then a long chord before they began, "*Happy Birthday…*" Once again the room was filled with happy singing. When the song was finished the girls once again played their signature phrase, nine notes played in lovely harmony.

In the days that followed the celebration, a surprising thing happened. Requests for both lessons and instruments tumbled in as well as many donated instruments. So many that Noell had to get a calendar just to keep track. There was even a mom who had taught tap dancing while she was in college that inquired about the possibility of offering a couple tap classes at Harmony House. The trio received requests from Emerald Valley, and Cedar Crest Retirement Centers and Dornbecker Children's Hospital. Caleb learned five or six popular Christmas carols that the girls could follow. Perhaps the most surprising request was from KGW channel 4, who wanted the girls to play short interludes that could be recorded and used as station breaks. The Program Director asked them why they played that brief nine note beginning. Cam answered, "It's just our way of testing that the violins are tuned together. They sound real bad if we don't keep them in tune with each other."

The profound occurrence following the celebration was the personal impact the audience received. Granted, there was no attending physician to verify the claims but still rumors or word of mouth accounts claimed more than a few amazing results. There were accounts of healings, both physical and emotional. One family was planning to file for divorce, but after the celebration they were convinced they could work it out. A man scheduled for back surgery claimed that the pain and numbness went away as the girls played their violins for their brother. A woman had a throat obstruction that was scheduled for surgery. She too astounded her physician with no sign of distress. A teenager, who was attending under protest because of her anger outbursts, became calm and appreciative of the girls. She even wanted to resume her music lessons so she could return to Harmony House. There were several more astounding claims of new strength or hope.

At Children's Hospital, where there were many attending physicians, the girls were invited to play their Christmas songs on the third and fourth floor; those are the cancer and recovery wards. After their tuning chords, they played a wonderful version of "*Ring Silver Bells*", which made listeners smile with joy. Then they played "*Angels We Have Heard on High*". The "*Gloria*" was so happy it seemed like two butterflies were dancing in sunshine. Finally they played, "*We Wish You a Merry Christmas*". At both ends of the long hallway they played again their tuning chords, even though most listeners would have welcomed many more songs. Curiously, doctors, nurses, anxious family, or those small bodies that were injured or ill, all felt an invigorating lift of energy and peace. One of the nurses commenting that for four days there was no fatality in the hospital, an unusual streak.

Kenny Fox announced that the residence level of Harmony House would be finished by December 15th on time and under budget. All the excess funds were being spent on landscaping and it would be fantastic. "I have a question for you," he said with a smile. "There's a large pile of rocks up by Murray Boulevard that seems a bit mysterious. If I didn't know better I'd guess it is a gravesite. But there is no marker or signs of any other. Before we tear into it, I thought I'd run it by you first. May I show it to you?"

They walked to the upper corner of the property, well out of the construction area. Kenny pointed to a mound of small boulders almost hidden by Black Berry vines and the high weeds. They circled the unusual collection before Kenny rolled the top one off. "They have been here a long time, I'll bet by the looks of it," he said as he rolled another. "It is too small for a grave, unless it is one for a child or a dog." The mound was about four or five feet across and three feet high, He rolled another heavy stone from the top. "Hey, there's a plank here. It looks like its hand hewn."

Michael began removing stones from the other side. Quickly they revealed that the plank was actually part of a carefully fashioned wooden tau cross, like a letter "T". There was another layer of smaller rocks below the cross, and below that there was a rotted canvas cover protecting a wood and brass case about two feet by a foot and a half, perhaps eight inches thick. The two men looked at each other with a bit of wonder and a lot more curiosity.

"Well, you're right. It's too small for a casket," Michael chuckled. "I wonder if this was placed here for safe-keeping or disposal."

Kenny replied, "I'm interested to see what's inside. Are you?"

Michael was already working to free the clasp that age and moisture had secured. "I'm even charmed by this box. It was not casually made." The pin was worked free and the hinge allowed him to gently open the lid. The box was filled with old papers.

"I don't recognize the language, do you Michael?" Kenny asked in confusion. "It looks sort of like German. What's this name? M. Simons, 1536? Oh my Lord!" Both men were studying the page for a minute or two. "Hey, what's going on?" he asked suddenly. The page seemed to lose clarity and then began to wrinkle. Without any contact the page disintegrated into a fine dust that ran off the next page like running water. They continued to stare until it happened again. Another page crumbled into dust and ran into the bottom of the box.

Reaching into his coat pocket for his own cell phone, Michael quickly said, "Kenny, use the photo feature on your cell phone. Let's capture this reaction" As he spoke another page was gone. For ten or twelve minutes they watched until all the pages were gone and the box was half filled with a powdery substance. Carefully Michael closed the box and reattached the clasp. Then looking at Kenny in wonder, he asked, "What the heck do you make of that? Have you ever seen such a self destruction?"

A befuddled expression underscored Kenny's response. "That felt like some sci-fi moment. I have never seen anything with that sort of a dry chemical reaction." He was quiet for just a moment, then added, "My dad-in- law is a chemistry professor at Portland State. I wonder if he could identify the substance we have captured in the box. Would you mind if I gave him a sample?"

"That's funny,' Michael replied. "I was just thinking about some contacts I have in government who might explore this. The trouble with the government is they quickly forget who they are serving and go off on their own merry way." He shook his head slightly. "I think I want someone who can examine these photo clips and explain what all those pages had to say. That's the mystery I'd like to know about."

"There is a pretty adequate language department at PS," Kenny offered. "I can ask Wayne, my dad-in-law, if he could find a translator." Kenny's relaxed smile demonstrated that he was enjoying this unexpected puzzle as much as Michael.

Christmas was nearly a non-event. Oh yes, the house was wonderfully decorated, a large tree adorned the alcove beside the grand piano and had a truckload of gifts under its boughs. Christmas music was non-stop in the festive home. For Noell and Michael it could not have been more complete. For the children, however, the fascination was with their musical instruments. Caleb probably spent five or six hours every day at the piano. The twins were even more charmed with their violins, especially after they heard Erin Copeland's Rodeo ballet and the Hoedown! The effort to duplicate the abandon and joy of the violins captivated the girls.

With most of the string section of the symphony orchestra involved with Harmony House, it was no surprise that Michael and Noell were popular attendees at the Portland Symphony New Year's gala. With several hundred of the area's outstanding music lovers in formal attire, it was a popular event. Several times during the evening Michael and Noell were sought out by appreciative parents or symphony supporters for their work with the youth. Two doctors from the Children's Hospital praised the twins' lovely Christmas melodies that were a blessing to the children.

And then, the conductor of the symphony, Kenneth Fromm, introduced himself. "My second chair said that you are popular, but I did not expect to stand in line to meet you," he said in greeting.

Michael was surprised at his negative reaction of the man's self absorbed arrogance.

"My Brandon has been invited to join the Harmony House class one strings as first chair. That's not surprising to me. He is a talented addition to any ensemble."

Michael tried to maintain a pleasant smile as he said, "I wasn't aware that Mr. Klein was recruiting more strings." What he really wanted to do was smack the cheesy smile in front of him.

"Oh my," the conductor said with a sigh. "If there is a youth symphony there must be a first chair, and I can't imagine a more talented person than Brandon for that position. You are so fortunate to have his consideration."

Michael saw Mr. Klein across the room and asked to be excused to talk shop with him. Actually, Michael had been studying the spots on Mr. Fromm's face that he wanted to swat.

Once they had exchanged greetings and praise for the evening's festivities, Michael asked, "Les is it true that you are recruiting section leaders for the youth symphony?" His expression was kindly but the question was fully armed.

"Oh crap, no!" Mr. Klein answered immediately. "I'll bet you have been talking to the biggest ego in the room. Fromm is quick to jump to conclusions and quicker to try to promote his kid to the same level of pompousness as he enjoys." He placed his hand on Michael's shoulder. "If I were choosing a first chair, I would consider Camilla before anyone else. But that is still a long way off. We haven't even met all the youngsters who will be part of it."

Michael thanked him for that unbiased attitude and looked around the room to find the lady he always wanted to be near.

New Year's Day dinner was a leisurely conversation about moving into the new residence in Harmony House. No one was eager to move, yet the children couldn't imagine any place more enjoyable than living there. They liked this house, but they loved every minute they were allowed to be in the music center. No move day was set, but the decision was made for sure.

Three days later when Michael drove over to pick up the girls after their first class lesson time, he found them both weeping.

"He took my violin," Cele was able to get out.

"Brandon stole it," Cam attested. "First he asked to borrow it and when she said 'no' he just walked out with it." Her tears were more under control, but just as intense.

Michael made a phone call to get the address and asked the girls to get in the car. It took only a few minutes to get to the Tigard home of the conductor. His aggressive knock on the door brought an immediate answer.

"Mrs. Fromm, may I speak with your husband or more to the point your pup Brandon?" His voice had the venom of disaster.

She was shaken by his lack of courtesy and realized this was a very angry man. "I'm afraid Brandon has not come home from his music lesson. His grandfather picks him up. They should be here soon. Would you like to wait?" Her soft voice faded to a whisper.

"Quit game-playing with me lady. Let me speak to your husband, then," Michael said stronger. "We have a very serious problem that is only going to be made worse by avoidance."

From the family room, a contrite man said. "It is Winter, isn't it? How can I help you?" He was dressed in workout clothes.

"Fromm, I don't need any help. I need the return of Celia's violin. Don't waste my time playing your ignorant games or you'll need an ambulance."

"I'm sure there must be some…."

Before he could finish the sentence, Michael's right hand grabbed a handful of the front of the man's shirt and a bit of hair and skin along with it. "I will not repeat myself. You are ten seconds from broken bones. Get the violin now, or so help me you will suffer." He didn't need to shout, the intensity was unmistakable.

Mrs. Fromm begged, "Please don't hurt him. The violin is upstairs in Brandon's room." She scurried away to fetch it.

"If it has a smudge on it, you will wear a bruise," Michael growled. "If there is a scratch on it you will bleed." Michael did not release his vice-like grip and Mr. Fromm knew it would do no good to struggle.

"Here it is!" Mrs. Fromm pleaded. "Please don't hurt him." She gently offered the case to Celia as a frightened boy looked down from his room.

The case, resting on the floor, was opened and the violin raised to her chin. Nine ascending notes were played and then four descending, a repeated single note and four ascending. It was not damaged.

"Daddy, it's not hurt. You can let him go." Then speaking to the men of the house the seven year old said in a voice far more mature, "You did a very bad thing. In case you feel like you are getting away with it, you will have a reminder in the morning and every morning until you apologize publicly to my violin."

Michael slowly released his grip. "Mr. Fromm I'm fairly certain you have a dark shadow now. I believe you will find it increasingly difficult to conduct the symphony. My suggestion is that you begin looking for a job in a different city. Perhaps in the meantime you can teach that spoiled whelp what it means to respect other people's property. He seems to be cursed with an inherited case of arrogance. This is not something that will just go away, nor bring either of you anything but grief."

All the while this brief confrontation was taking place, Cam remained a silent witness. She was very proud of her twin's spunky willingness to be in the midst of it. But more she pondered her own fierce love for a warrior father who had again and again rescued them from danger and brought immediate justice.

At the supper table Cam was giving her mom an account of the incident. "Daddy grabbed his shirt and I was sure it was going to be very bad for Mr. Fromm. His wife ran upstairs to get the violin. They all knew that it was weasel Brandon who had stolen it." Looking at Cele, she asked, "How come you played our tuning notes?"

"I don't know. I wanted to be sure she wasn't damaged and she told me what to play." The smiling twin had no better reason for her choice.

Finally, Noell reminded the kids that they had school work to get done before bedtime, regardless of what the violin said. In the cozy darkness of their bed, however, she revisited the account with Michael. "Thank you once again for resolving a problem for my children. You are without a doubt their super hero." She embraced him in a comfortable way.

The contented husband turned toward her to enjoy her familiar warmth. "I don't know about that. You should have seen Cele. If I was Fromm I'd be more worried about her threat than whatever I might have said or done. She told him it would be bad for him until he publicly apologizes to the violin. It sort of made my skin crawl, she was so intense."

Noell scooted in a bit closer and said softly, "I love to make your skin crawl."

At breakfast there was no comment about yesterday's troubles. But there was a lot of conversation about the possibility of moving to a new home. Each one of them admitted that this house was quite comfortable. The prospect of living in Harmony House, however, was nearly magical! The vote was unanimous to move as soon as possible.

At the Fromm house the vote was also unanimous. Both dad and Brandon needed to see the doctor and Clare knew it. On Tuesday morning they both had a boil under their chin. The painful infections had appeared during the night. Initial phone conversations with their physician had suggested that warm moist clothes and antibiotics would produce comfort and healing of the furuncle within a couple weeks. On Wednesday morning there was an additional one on Kenneth's hand and on Brandon's cheek. On Thursday morning Kenneth's cheek and Brandon's forehead had new infections. The outbreaks were swollen, red and very painful. Their doctor explained that furunculosis was contagious as a staphylococcus of the hair follicles. Hospitalization was suggested until the source of the bacteria could be isolated and controlled.

By the following Tuesday afternoon the face and body of both infected Fromm's had four new outbreaks. Angry swollen boils were growing larger by the day. A tearful wife and mother drove her patients to Harmony House where Mr. Klein was teaching the first class violins. The desperate trio interrupted the class which was alarmed by the swollen and deformed faces of both the conductor and his son.

"Please forgive us," Mrs. Fromm pleaded toward Celia. "Please." Her voice trembled with desperation.

Quietly Celia answered, "You came into our house and broke a trust. You took the most precious thing I own. If you kneel down and apologize to my violin I will forgive you." She held out her white violin.

Kenneth Fromm, conductor of the Portland Symphony murmured "We are sorry for the inconvenience we caused you." His face was a mess of swollen infections.

The auditorium was in shocked silence. No one had ever witnessed such a dramatic moment as the revered conductor and the second grader silently stared at each other. Finally Celia stood and placed her violin in its case saying, "You are not sorry enough to apologize. Come back next week when you have seven more and these start to break open. Then we'll see if you really are sorry." She turned to leave the stage.

Mrs. Fromm nearly screamed, "No, Kenneth, what in the world is wrong with you. For God's sake apologize. Brandon you selfish little turd, get on your knees and apologize, or I promise to God, you will walk home to an empty house. Both of you mental midgets are responsible for this mess! Now make it right!" She was near hysterics.

Brandon was crying as he knelt and said, "Celia, I took your violin even after you told me not to. I am sorry and I promise I will never take anything again." He didn't know what words to use, but he hoped those were enough.

Celia stopped and turned. Opening her case she held out her violin. "Say it to her, Brandon," was all she said.

Crying even harder, Brandon blurted, "I apologize. I'm very sorry I took you away from Celia. I will never do it again." He put his head down on the floor.

She looked at the conductor for a long moment. When it seemed he was not going to respond, she started to close the case.

"No, wait," he said painfully. "I didn't know he was going to do it, but when he brought the violin home I didn't fuss. We both played it and I'm as guilty as Brandon. I apologize. I'm ashamed of our behavior and ask for your forgiveness." Tears were running down his face.

Celia looked at Camilla, who only nodded.

Celia said, "She forgives you both. I do too, but I don't want to ever play with you again. Please don't come back here." The twins raised their violins and together played a nine note tuning cord.

Now who's to say what just happened for sure? For those who witnessed that brief encounter, not much actually happened. A modest discrepancy was corrected. But to the class members who understood, the solemn strength of the twins who could actually black-list the conductor was apparent. To Mrs. Fromm, who now saw her husband and son in much less favor, or to Mr. Klein who shuddered with comprehension, this redemptive moment would profoundly affect their lives forever. To the twins there was verification of what they had suspected. The violins were not simply spiritless inanimate instruments. To the two who had received forgiveness, there was a realization that healing of those painful boils had mercifully begun.

A few minutes later the girls opened the door to see if their mom was there to take them home. To their surprise she was standing by a long black car, talking with the strange lady that had donated their violins. Their mom motioned for them to join the conversation at the car. "Girls," she said, "This is Mrs. Gleason, the lady who donated your marvelous violins." There were hellos and words of appreciation again. "Mrs. Gleason stops in every now and then to listen to your lessons," their mom reported. "She thinks you are doing very well."

A soft voice from within the car said, "Celia, Camilla, you have demonstrated the wisdom in your selection. I am very proud of the progress you are making. You have learned a major lesson for ones so young. You can defend the violins. Your courage and fortitude were remarkable. Next you will probably learn that they can defend you as well. Don't be afraid to call upon them if you need help and your brave Papa is not nearby. The strength of the violins will be yours as well."

As before, the girls didn't know what to make of her words, but they had been spoken with such sincerity they knew that they should remember them.

As the black car drove away, Les Klein was turning out the lights and locking the doors of Harmony House, concluding another satisfying lesson time. He was about to call to Noell. Michael had requested a list of available instruments for the orchestra, and another list of those that were still needed to begin the junior symphony. Instead, he shouted a warning to her. Out of the dark parking lot a car was rushing straight at the three standing in the shadows! Its headlights were not on and there seemed to be no intent to brake.

"Noell, look out!" was all he could scream.

Perhaps it was his warning, or perhaps she heard the rush of the oncoming car. She had only time to glance at the danger and give the twins a protective shove. They and their violin cases went tumbling out of harm's way. The bumper of the car, however, caught her leg with a sickening thump, knocking her several feet to the side. The car swerved at the last moment, colliding with a huge landscape boulder. There was a pop of airbags deploying and then everything was still.

Les was running to give assistance and at the same time calling 911. He was sure there would be injuries needing an ambulance. The musician in him also worried about the condition of the violins. He had watched the cases land hard on the concrete sidewalk. The twins were crying, but more from fear than injury. Their mom was lying still but her eyes were open and she seemed alert and in pain. He jerked open the passenger door of the car. With instant recognition he shouted, "Kenneth, for God's sake, what were you thinking?" The blood covered face of the director looked at him with confusion and shame. Beside him a stunned wife was bleeding from glasses that broke when the airbag slammed against her face and in the back seat a son who had not secured his seatbelt before the encounter with the boulder was whimpering. It was a mess.

The police cruiser must have been close when they got the call, because they were at Harmony House within three minutes. The ambulance was only moments behind them, and Michael was only moments after that. The initial evaluation suggested that the twins' only injuries were a couple skinned knees. Noell's head had hit the sidewalk pretty hard. They suspected a concussion but the more painful injury was to her knee and leg. A dark contusion suggested broken blood vessels and the loose motion was symptomatic of a torn ligament or meniscus. To minimize further injury her leg was stabilized with an air splint. She would be taken to Cedar Hills Hospital for X-rays. Mrs. Fromm was given a couple butterfly bandages and the advice to see her primary care physician in the morning. Kenneth Fromm attempted to declare the cause of the accident was a mechanical malfunction, but the tirade of his wife was more believable by the police. He was arrested on three charges of aggravated assault and his car was impounded as evidence. By the time he would finally be a free man, he would be the former conductor of the Portland Symphony and the former husband of Clare Fromm. Oh the staggering cost of vanity.

When Mr. Klein retrieved the violin cases, he was amazed to find no evidence of damage to either the cases or the instruments they carried, not a single scratch! The leather coverings seemed as fresh as new ones. All the while a relieved father was comforting his twins, assuring them that any injury was minor and their mom would be just fine. He was surprised when Cam embraced him and asked if they could accompany their mom to the hospital.

"That's a kind thought Sweetie," Michael said softly. "But she'll be in the emergency room where there are many people and we might be in the way or a distraction." He felt that was a sufficient answer and a truthful explanation.

"But Daddy, there is someone else there who needs to hear the violins too." Cam's blue eyes were steady on his as she spoke. "And the doctors appreciate their help."

There were six beds in the Cedar Hills Emergency room, only one of which was occupied before the folks from Harmony House arrived. He was a frail elderly man who was unaware of their presence. Mr. Fromm was placed in bed six where a duty officer could keep guard. Noell was given some pain relief and placed in bed one awaiting X-rays. The doctor smiled his approval when diminutive Cam asked if they could quietly play their violins for their mom's comfort.

The girls had played all of "*It Is Well with My Soul*" and "*I need Thee Every Hour*" before their mom was wheeled into the examination room. She had only been gone a couple minutes when Cam asked her daddy if she could speak with the doctor.

"What do you need Sweetie?" he asked gently.

She smiled weakly saying, "The man next to us wants to tell Jesse a secret." She was sure it was a puzzle, but equally convinced her daddy would accept the request.

The doctor returned moments later with Michael. "Did you hear Mr. Phipps say something?" he asked her softly.

"It's sort of a puzzle," Cam began not knowing where this was leading. "He gave an idea to my violin who gave it to me. He has a secret he wants me to give to his son Jesse." Her innocent face gave no indication of confusion.

"I don't understand," the doctor began with a bit of a head shake. "How do you know Jed Phipps or his son?"

"I don't know them. I said he gave his idea to my violin when we played. She gave the idea to me. He said it was very important though." It was amazing how fragile she appeared and yet how strong.

The doctor stood up still shaking his head in confusion. "I don't understand what's going on, but Jesse Phipps is in the cafeteria getting a bit of supper. You'll find him there. He is by himself wearing a blue sport coat. His dad has been comatose for several hours so I can't imagine how you might have communicated with him."

The trio had no trouble identifying Jesse, but there was a bit of confusion as Cam tried to convince him that she had a secret to tell him. He was dubious at first, assuming this might be some intrusive request for a hand-out. When he finally bent down near her, she whispered, "In your daddy's desk in the bottom left drawer under the magazines there is a false bottom. In it you will find the bank papers that show Pam has been cheating and the pill bottle she has given your daddy. Make sure you have a policeman with you to receive the evidence. There is still time to help your daddy, but not much. That's all he told my violin." Jesse was shocked with comprehension. She had described his father's desk accurately and she knew about Pam. She looked into his brown eyes so intently that he was convinced of the moment's urgency. Doing the only logical thing in light of this information he thanked her and rushed out of the cafeteria. If there was any possible validity to this puzzle he would not waste the opportunity.

By the time they got back to bed number one, their mom was there with a smile. "The doctor says there is too much swelling to determine the extent of the injury. For sure there is some tissue damage and a greenstick fracture, a little crack in the bone. He'll put on a soft cast and we can go home. Isn't that good news? We can come back in a couple days to talk about repairing the knee."

While they waited the girls played "*There's Something About That Name*" and "*Take Time To Be Holy*," which exhausted their sacred selections. Michael was pretty impressed with all the songs of faith they did know. To his knowledge they had not been in a church. Little did they know that there was yet another still listener in bed two who heard and greatly benefited from the serenade.

A few minutes later they were preparing to leave when a burst of activity filled bed two. An intravenous drip was inserted that would neutralize and reverse the poison Mr. Phipps had been given. His son reported happily that his dad was going to pull through. He held Cam's smiling face, "Thanks to you, young lady! I think I'm falling in love. I don't know how in the world you knew, but you were very brave to tell me. It was just as you said and the explanation of a lot of trouble we have been having. I'm afraid my sister, who has a terrible drug addiction, has burned some big bridges and will be in prison for a while. Maybe it will be a time for her to clean up her life and regain control of it. We hope so." He kissed her forehead saying, "Thank you again. If you will tell me where, I'd like to send you some flowers." Michael was glad to offer him a business card for Harmony House.

Jesse continued. "Dad said it was a strange feeling. It was like he was sinking into darkness and he was helpless. Then he heard your violins. They were like small candles that chased away the darkest shadow. They brought him hope and new strength to hold on. The doctor thinks he will be here recuperating for a couple days. But he is awake, alert and on the mend for sure. He wants to tell you later how grateful he is. I'm just glad he is going to get better, thanks to you." He gave both girls a little hug and shook Michael's and Noel's hands. It was obvious that he was bubbling over with gladness.

Caleb was listening for the garage door to open. Then he rushed out to greet his mom and sisters, even though his dad had called three times to update him on the hospital activities. "Is it true that he tried to run over all of you?" he asked, already sure of the answer.

Cele was eager to tell the entire account, beginning with the conductor's apology but her mom intervened, insisting it was still a school night and there would be ample time in the morning. As they made their way into the house and prepared for bed, the lad was sure once again that his family was unique. They could stand in the midst of an emergency and handle it with grace and efficiency. The admiration he had for his dad was even more complicated. The gentle thoughtful funny side of him had won their hearts completely. The no-prisoners combative side of him gave Caleb haunting dreams and memories. He knew that he loved and respected his hero dad deeply. Yes, theirs was a unique family. It made him shiver a bit with pride, and some apprehension.

When Michael took Noell back to the orthopedist to determine the extent of her injuries, they were each surprised by his diagnosis. The swelling was gone, the big bruise was now only a green reminder of which knee had been hit by the car and there was no sign of a fracture or pain whatsoever. She had full range of motion and strength. There was no evidence of knee damage. The doctor asked, "Are you the same woman I examined Tuesday evening?"

Noell smiled sweetly and said, "I guess I'm a swift healer." But she exchanged a glance with Michael which implied there was more of a mystery here than speedy healing.

The house was listed for sale and the third family to look at it offered full price. They were charmed by it too, because their daughter loved the piano alcove and the idea of Harmony House. The transition for both families was smooth and accomplished by the first of February.

A similar transition was making Les Klein's life more enjoyable. He had accepted an employment contract as manager of the Harmony House music program. "Start small and let it grow slowly," Michael had instructed. "We want this place to be safe and fun for young music makers." The goal was to create a music center where children could find instruction for learners and participation in a variety of ensembles for the more accomplished students with the ultimate objective of creating a youth symphony. The job gave him unexpected additional income as well as recognition in the community without interrupting his commitment to the Portland Symphony. It was all good!

"Michael Love, may I ask you a question?" It was her way of presenting a chore or favor that she wanted.

"That is a question," he chuckled. "What else is on your mind?" He absolutely loved this playful and gentle woman.

"Well, in my last letter to mom, I told her about these new facilities. She was never in the California house. Heinrich made it pretty clear that he didn't have time for my folks. It's been almost five years since they saw their grandchildren. Since we have the guest suite now, would you mind if I invite them for a visit? I miss them a lot." She made a sad face as though her words hadn't been convincing enough.

With a wide smile he answered, "Said another way, our children have missed out on five years of extended family and the spoiling attention that only a grandparent can offer. I'm surprised the kids haven't filed a formal complaint. Of course your folks should be with us. When would you like to invite them?"

She hadn't expected it would be that easy. It was just another example of how much Michael loved her and the kids. "The twins' birthday is four days before Easter. I was hoping they could be here long enough to do both."

"Maybe we could suggest that Les plans another Fancy Fiddles about then," Michael added. "That would be a wonderful way for your folks to see the talent of the kids." He wanted to make sure there was no doubt about his support of her idea.

A couple hours later, Kenny had another interesting suggestion. "Michael, have you got a minute?" he asked. When he knew he had his attention, the contractor asked, "I remember you called the empty second floor space a possible food court. Can we think about that for a minute or two? Have you made any decisions about it?"

When Michael shook his head with a bit of a shrug, he answered, "I guess I imagined something that could be more convenient when there were more people around to support it."

"Have you noticed how many folks are in the auditorium listening to the classes? It's not a whole bunch now, but it is growing, and if Les gets that youth symphony organized I'll bet there will be a lot more. Cheryl has this idea." He took a big breath knowing that once again he was depending on Michael's good nature. "If we would finish the kitchen area with a dish washer, refrigerator and stove, we could start a deli sort of food bar; you know, sandwiches, coffee and sodas, maybe even milkshakes. She would be happy to operate it a few hours about lunchtime each day. With a dozen or so tables and chairs. it could be a good place for parents to wait during lessons too." That was probably enough of the idea to get a first notion.

Michael was still for a moment thinking what a good idea Kenny was offering. He didn't want to say "yes" too quickly. He did ask "I don't suppose we will need a building permit, will we? But for sure we'll need some sort of food handler's license. Can you take care of that? When Kenny nodded with a grin, Michael added, "I suppose you will need to finish those restrooms and fashion a storage closet." He thought for another moment. "A small office space where Sammy can have a cradle would also be nice. He might as well come along with mom." With one more moment to make sure, he said, "O.K. here's the deal. You order the appliances and counters we'll need and any subs you need for electrical or plumbing. Just give me the bill and I'll take care of it. Cheryl can run it whatever hours she chooses. The first six months are a trial period, rent free. She pays for supplies and keeps whatever profit there might be. In July we will find an agreeable contract. Run that by her and if she agrees, you can begin at your convenience. Agreed?"

"You bet!" Kenny said practically laughing as he held out his hand. "I was ready to pay for the set-up, but I guess it is your place, and your privilege to make the investment."

"I know that if you do the work, it will be done correctly. Just tell Cheryl that my favorite cookie is a Snicker Doodle. If she fixes some, I'm sure to be a steady customer. You know, I live nearby." They shared the laughter and confidence that this would be a positive step for the Harmony House.

When Michael asked Les Klein if there would be a possibility of a Fancy Fiddles II, there was immediate enthusiasm for the opportunity to demonstrate a year of dynamic growth. "We have the entire string section for the youth symphony and two string quartets. There are guitars and flutes that would welcome exposure. Oh my yes! Let's schedule the Wednesday before Easter. School will be out that week, which will probably take away two or three. But the majority of students will delight at an evening of recital." His expression was very plain to see. It also would happen. He began to choose both sacred and classical music selections that could demonstrate the development of Harmony House musicians.

The weeks slid by orderly but at an increasing pace. The 10th of March was written on a host of eager calendars. Surely none were more excited than the Winters'.

Finally Kenny hung a sign announcing *Intermission Deli* was open for business. The Fancy Fiddle II folders were printed and the musicians were rehearsed. And it was time to meet mom and dad Frost at the airport. On the way there, Noell cautioned Michael to be patient with her stepfather. "He is pretty opinionated about most things even though he knows little about them. I avoid politics unless I just want to fight with him." Her sly smile suggested that she had done that often. With a confident smile, Michael assured her that a Winter and a Frost would never have a problem. They waited by the appropriate baggage carousel until Noell spotted them, then ran to greet her folks.

On the way to West Hills, Noell was trying to be a tour guide, pointing out first the Columbia River, and then the seven bridges of Portland over the Willamette River. Her dad said, "It must rain a lot here with all these rivers." Noell answered, "I'm told it rains less here than in Minneapolis." They were almost to Aloha when Ed asked Michael, "Did I hear that you were a security guard or watchman before you met our girl?"

"Yes sir," Michael answered with a smile. "In fact, I was unemployed at the time we met. A placement agent thought I might be able to help her."

"I guess you did," the dad said. "It sounds like you helped yourself too, now that you are married to a rich widow." His tone was not quite abrasive, but close to it.

With a cheery voice, Michael said, "I give thanks to my lucky star every day. This lady has made me so happy I want to whistle."

He would have said more but Noell interrupted saying, "O.K. Bully Boys, play nice together. Dad, Michael is humble enough not to tell you all of our first meeting. I was hiding with the kids in the agent's home because Heinrik had threatened to kill us." There was a bit of a gasp from the back seat. "Michael dispatched two armed men who broke into her house, then he took us all to the Marine Base on Coronado Island in San Diego, where we could be safe while he took care of the rest of the problem. I won't bore you with the details but by the time I could convince this awesome man to marry me there were nine dead French soldiers of fortune who had been hired to kill me and the children; Heinrik, his brother Phillip and four of his body guards were dispatched as well. They had kidnapped the kids in an attempt to switch identities. Finally the attorney who masterminded the whole mess got put down too. He died of a heart attack while we were talking with him in his office. Michael was a Special Forces Marine Chief Warrant Officer for 13 years. And before you embarrass yourself by suggesting that he has married me for my money, I can tell you that he retrieved nearly twenty million dollars that had been swindled from our investment account. That and all my other investments as well as the money from the sale of the mansion, is securely invested in federal bonds and he has accepted not one dime from me. He wrote a check from his own bank account for the house we have lived in and another for the facility we have now, called Harmony House. The children adore him almost as much as I do. He has truly redeemed our lives. I think you'll like him too when you get to know him." The car was silent for the final part of their journey. That was a lot of information to process.

As Michael turned into the Harmony House parking lot. Ed said, "It looks nice. Are these apartments?"

"No dad, this is Harmony House. Downstairs is a music auditorium where the kids have their music lessons. We live upstairs." Noell could see her dad struggling to grasp the scope of it. They drove around to the back where a garage door opener moved the steel gate. "The elevator up to the foyer is at the far end of the parking garage. Ours is here by the freight elevator." She was enjoying this reveal a lot.

"Are there many stairs?" Ed asked a bit bewildered. "Neither Helen or I can manage many stairs these days."

Noell asked more concerned, "Is your heart giving you trouble again?"

"No," her dad answered a little out of breath just thinking about it. "I've been suffering from Emphysema and your mom's Arthritis is getting worse. We're a pair of old folks you know."

Michael had their bags out of the trunk and placed a card and code into the elevator, which opened immediately. When the doors opened upstairs, they were in their home. Michael offered to take their coats and asked if they had eaten before they left Chicago. When Ed shook his head Michael beamed, "Great! I haven't had a chance to sample Cheryl's Deli. Let's go into the food court and see what's available." The parents were staring at the remarkable modern open interior. Truly this was beyond their imagination. "Let's leave your stuff here for a while. Then we'll show you your rooms on the west side. The kids are in the middle sort of, and we are on the east side. It's pretty splendid, wouldn't you agree." For once Ed was truly speechless.

There were seven or eight tables with lunch folks when they entered the food court. Cheryl waved a greeting and told Noell that Kenny had been helping with sandwiches. "So far the most popular one has been the Turkey Cranberry with cream cheese, but the meat loaf is a close second. We've been pretty busy for the past two hours." Orders were taken and the folks found a table near the west windows, which allowed a bit of scattered sunshine to warm them.

"This is…." Helen was fishing for a descriptive word, "amazing, spectacular and oh so unique. Can you tell me how this all works?"

Noell said beaming a happy smile, "Well the concept began when Michael saw the possibility in this partially constructed building that was bankrupt. He wondered if we could build an auditorium style music center where the kids could meet new friends and enjoy their talents."

Her dad interrupted, asking, "And he just wrote a check for it all?"

With her pixie smile she said "Yup. Then I wondered if we could create a comfortable living space with this empty upstairs. The contractor and architect gave me lots of choices. It was so fun to think what we could do with all this space. It is so open and light with all these windows. The media room has a flat screen TV and a dozen comfy chairs."

"Cheryl is a new mom and wife of our contractor. She requested use of this final part of the upstairs. Michael set up a tab for our kids so they can have chocolate milk and cookies after school. With the Fancy Fiddles tomorrow night there is a bunch of activity here this afternoon. I'm impressed with her menu. Hey, here comes our sandwiches."

Before the food was served, Ed asked, "You mean to tell me that you own this whole damned thing?"

Michael leaned over a bit to answer, "We would prefer to think of it as a blessed thing." They enjoyed sandwiches and chips that felt and tasted wonderfully homemade and Cheryl added a sample plate of Snicker Doodles!

They were just leaving the food court when Mr. Klein came in. A very large smile bloomed on his face as he approached Michael. "I'm glad to catch you," he beamed. "We've just had a marvelous dress rehearsal. It's going to be a sensational program. You'll be very proud of Harmony House." The smile faded a bit. "That Lewis lady came back for a follow-up interview. I told her we had distributed over a hundred instruments and have over a hundred and twenty children in one class or another. She asked who was paying my salary and where were the funds coming from. I told her she had been warned about trying to stick her nose in other people's affairs and informed her that KOIN was going to be broadcasting the programs from now on. She asked what were we hiding and I asked her if she made all of her financial information public. She left in a huff, but I think she'll be back tomorrow evening because her daughter is playing in the second class."

The kids came in just then, having finally finished their longer music lessons. They were going to have major parts in the Fancy Fiddles tomorrow night. They were eager to meet their grandparents, after they collected snacks from Miss Cheryl that is.

Introductions were made to people the kids either had never met (in the case of the twins) or had no recollection. Caleb had only been two. There was a rush of praise and compliments until Grandpa Ed asked if they missed California. The three children looked at him with disbelief and Noell asked, "Dad, were you listening to our account of last year?"

He answered sheepishly, "Well you know, I'm so da.... so very nervous to meet these darling grandchildren I didn't know what to ask." Laughter covered his embarrassment.

Noell suggested, "Let's go back in the house. We can take a quick look around and I'm sure the children would like to play for you."

The tour began at the elevators. Noell said, "We call this the gathering room, or living room." It was pretty formal with sofa and chairs and a lovely view to the north toward the city. Here's your room. There are two bedrooms and a bathroom. If you want a tub, let me know, there is a jetted tub in our room. All the other bathrooms have showers. Right next door is another guest room just like yours."

Moments later she introduced them to the family room and media room. "The kids love to watch TV, but so far we only watch the news and a couple other boring channels."

"Here's a nice guest bathroom, and the girls each have a room with a shared bathroom. There are pocket doors from each side."

"There at the end of the hall that goes into the food court there is an empty space we haven't decided about . It might be for a live-in housekeeper if Michael has his way. Right now it's just storage."

"Caleb's room is on the other side of the hallway. He also has a bathroom. Here on the corner is the music room with the piano and enough room for several music makers."

"Then is our room, which is just like yours except we have a tub. The office is at the end. The dining area is there on the east corner and of course the kitchen. The laundry room is there by the elevators. We're never sure where Alice and Amanda might choose to sleep, but their food and potty box are in the laundry room. They are pretty spoiled kitties and bless us with some affection only when the girls are around. The door next to the coat closet is an emergency stairway in case of a power outage. There's another one of those from the food court."

"You know, it's funny. I lived in a 12 million dollar Hollywood Hills mansion which was not anywhere close to as nice as this place."

Grandpa Ed asked quietly, "And it's all paid for and all yours?"

"Yup," was all Noell could happily say.

The parents strolled through a second look while the kids were getting ready for their private presentations. When they were all ready, the twins began with a nine note tuning cord and then went into Beethoven's *"Joyful, Joyful."* Caleb joined them on the second verse adding power and additional harmony. The trio played a couple patriotic songs and finished with *"It Is Well with My Soul."* The adults were charmed by their talent; yes, charmed indeed.

Before retiring to their suite for the night, Helen gave Noell a happy hug, saying, "Thank you for this wonderful day. My heart is filled with love and admiration for you all. It must be this clean Portland air. After this long day, Ed and I are amazed at the energy we are feeling . He is breathing so much more freely he didn't need his nebulizer and I am pain-free for the first time in months." She gave both Noell and Michael a tender kiss goodnight.

Oh my goodness, Mr. Klein did such a fantastic job with the Fancy Fiddle program! The auditorium was filled; fifty chairs were brought down from the food court and another fifty folks were standing in the side aisles. He graciously welcomed the crowd and thanked Harmony House for their generous support. A very brief explanation of the number of children and teachers involved this past year was followed immediately by the entire string section playing, *"It's a Grand Old Flag."*

Each class had prepared a special melody to play. The third classes played familiar children's songs. The second classes showed growth and development. The first classes were inspiring talent. Finally it was time for the twin pianos of Caleb and Carrey James with the twin violins playing *"Gloria, Gloria"*, a four part canon from the Community of Taize. That feature combination played *"Bring Him Home"* from Les Miserable's, and the evening ended with the twin violins playing *"Sometimes When It Rains"* from the Secret Garden. The nine note cord was almost lost in the standing applause, which was an invitation for the entire group to play an encore led by Mr. Klein's violin: *"My Country 'tis of Thee."* The happy audience sang along with gusto. What a show! Mr. Klein received a standing ovation as well. The entire troupe of musicians stood and took a bow. It was one of those moments that most of the children would remember. For Caleb, Celia and Camilla it was a moment they would remember as a highlight of childhood.

The folks who made their contented way out of Harmony House gave little thought to the nature of the building, whether it was a commercial auditorium or a private opportunity. But for those who recognized the founder, who was now diligently replacing the chairs from the food court, it was an opportunity to thank him and praise his commitment to a vital youth program. The auditorium was nearly empty when he noticed a lone person sitting quietly. His first thought was that she had fallen asleep. Just as quickly he wondered if she had a medical emergency, so he approached her carefully.

"Ma'am are you O.K.?" he asked softly.

The familiar face turned toward him with a warm smile. "Yes, Papa, I'm simply enjoying the echo of achievement. You have accomplished more in the last year than even the most optimistic could imagine. Well done, sir." Her smile remained as she added, "The twins are also far ahead of schedule. Their service at the hospital was heroic, and accomplished with pure innocence. They are remarkable. I am grateful that after such violence in your past there can be this season of blessed peace. Well done, sir."

Michael sat next to her and turned so he could see her face. Her reference to violence was a bit too personal for comfort. "Mrs. Gleason, may I call you Elva?" he asked politely. "We have seen some amazing moments in the presence of the violins. Can you tell me about them. Is there any reason I should be on guard for the girl's safety?" His gaze was direct and she thrilled again in the memory of her own father.

"Believe me sir," she answered with respect. "The violins are powerful, as you are. And like you, they have been designed for doing good, enabling justice and practicing mercy wherever possible. You continue to do the excellent task of being a loving father and they will help. It makes my heart glad that you can be direct enough to ask me this. It shows me that you are sincere at heart as well as brave. We will be admirers for a while if you will allow us. I think soon you will have helpful information." She took a deep breath and Michael anticipated that their conversation was over. Then she said very softly, "You know that God's most powerful angel was also named Michael. You have a favored namesake." She rose with some difficulty saying, "Goodnight sir. I hope I have the privilege of hearing those violins again soon."

Michael reached into his pocket for a business card. Offering it to her, he said, "Call us whenever you would like to have them play for you. They love any audience."

She didn't take the card but said, "Thank you again. You may hear from us again soon." Slowly she made her way out to the long black car at the curb. Michael had a bunch to tell Noell for sure.

The house was still buzzing with excitement from the program. Each person had praise to share. It was most fun hearing Cele compliment her brother for the leadership in the canon. "You started us so strong and Carrey picked it right up. We were just trying to match you! It was so fun! Don't you love how Carrey watches you?" Her excited voice rattled along. "I don't think even Disney Land was as much fun as tonight! Did you see how everybody stood up and clapped for us?" Somewhere about then her dad came in. Immediately she flew into his arms saying, "It was so fun, daddy. Thank you!"

Cam and Caleb joined in the hug, saying about the same thing. Finally Noell broke it up by offering her Applesauce Pecan pie with ice cream. After all a fun program deserves a fun treat. Then it was the grandparents' turn to give accolades, "That program was worth the whole trip. I couldn't believe the talent of you three. It was like I was watching professionals playing," Ed said with enthusiasm.

"We couldn't be more proud!" Helen added with a nod.

By the time the plates were cleaned the subject of tomorrow's agenda was bounced around. "We have a couple fun suggestions" Michael began. "Snowy Mt. Hood is about an hour east of us. Timberline Lodge still has skiing and the lodge is a great place for lunch. Or if we go about forty five minutes west we could visit Seaside, the Pacific Ocean end of the Lewis and Clark trail. Do either of those sound inviting?"

Helen answered almost immediately, "Where will the children be? Will they go with us?"

"We can all go in the Range Rover," he replied. "But since there is no school this week, Mr. Klein has been taking advantage of it by inviting all the first class violins and of course Caleb and Carrie to some special planning for another recital evening. These kids are really plugged into music. I think they will be right here all day. That's another feature of the food court. They would rather order something from Miss Cheryl than have their mom cook. So a third option is that you can visit the auditorium as much as you like." His warm smile underscored the options.

Ed offered a plan. "We're flying home next Wednesday. Do you think we could put off the beach until Monday or Tuesday when the kids are back in school? We've seen enough snow this winter."

In the darkness of their bedroom, Noell snuggled against Michael. "Do you remember asking me if I would favor immersing the children in music? We were hoping they would find some friends. Remember?"

I do recall the conversation," he replied with a smile she could not see but was sure it was there.

Noell whispered, "I think neither of us had a clue that something like this could happen. Do you think it was just meant to be?" She was aware of his warmth and strength.

"I don't know what that means," he softly answered. "I guess I believe that there are always potentials around us. If we take advantage of one of them and feed it with enough resources, amazing things like this can happen." His hand slid down her side and stroked in a way that was sure to catch her attention.

"I guess you don't want to talk about it, huh?" She turned a bit more toward him and demonstrated that she didn't either.

The morning news reported that during the night a fire had done significant damage to the century old Aloha Christian Church. Apparently an unattended candle had ignited a pile of papers. Without fire suppression, the blaze had enough time to spread into the wooden walls and sanctuary floor joists. The church was unusable until a full structural evaluation could be conducted.

"What a shame," Helen sighed. "They can't have Easter in their church. I'll bet there are a lot of disappointed folks."

It was a good thing that those at the table couldn't hear Michael's thoughts: "Carelessness demands a price. Too bad some kid's negligence has cost them a reconstruction bill. It will probably be a better place when it's repaired, and insurance will pay for most of it." There was little sympathy for those folks who had a deep emotional attachment to the old building, or those who wondered if it was their carelessness that that had caused the fire. It would not be a stretch of the truth to say that grace was not an operative word in Michael's dictionary, except in matters concerning his family of course.

When the phone rang he had a strange instant thought that it was Mrs. Gleason calling. Then as quickly he envisioned the charred church. "Good morning, this is Michael," he answered.

"Good morning sir," the male voice said, "I'm Rusty James. Our kids are part of your music program. I'm calling this morning because you probably heard the news about the church fire last night. I'm on the emergency committee seeking a temporary place for us to hold our Easter worship. We have a congregation of about three hundred. Our daughter, Carrey, suggested I inquire if you ever let others use your auditorium."

Without knowing why, Michael liked this man. He had identified himself and his purpose clearly and waited to see if there would be a reply. "Rusty." Michael began with a kind voice, "I'm sorry for your challenge. I'll tell you that Harmony House is pretty new, so we have a short history to work with. My first response is that we have an adequate seating capacity for sure. But as quickly I am aware that we do not have classrooms or nursery facilities of any sort for children. We are a music venue."

"I understand sir. This morning we are only trying to reconnoiter our possibilities for Pastor Carlson. The church nursery was not damaged at all. We are about five blocks east of your location. Would you consider our use of the auditorium if there were no preschool children?" There was a quiet tone of hope in Rusty's voice.

"For the sake of discussion I would be favorable to that," Michael said with a chuckle. "Rusty do I detect a bit of military in your voice?"

"Yes sir," the instant response came firm and sure. "I was in the Marine Corps from '93 to '97, with five tours to Iraq." There was a courteous pause and he replied, "I think I hear the same quality from you, sir."

"Semper fi, I was NSA Special Forces from '94 to '07, mostly drug interdiction. But before we get all warm and fuzzy, I suppose you are on a short time line. Get back to me and let me know if we should work out the details. It's been good talking to you Rusty."

"Same here, sir. Regardless of what happens with the church, I would be glad to know more about Harmony House and how I could be of assistance. Good day sir."

When he returned to the table, he shared the nature of the phone request. Noell immediately said, "When we built this we never considered the possibility it could serve the community in a time of emergency. I'm happy they thought to call us."

Ed's response was, "Yeah, you better watch out. You know what they say: when the camel gets his nose inside the tent, before you know it the tent is full of humps and hairy legs." A sly smile suggested that the hairy legs part was funny to him.

Helen said softly as though she was speaking only to herself, "Maybe if we refuse to go to church, it eventually finds a way to come to us."

Caleb said, "I can't believe Carrey is bringing her whole church to Harmony House. I wonder if it will change us." Each person at the table had a different interpretation of his question.

Cam said, "I wonder if the violins will help them too?" Once again her question had a variety of answers.

Before noon Rusty called back, "Thank you, Mr. Winter, for your consideration. The Golf course has room enough for us but no piano and limited parking. We also must be gone by noon because they have a full tee time scheduled. They did ask for $500 for the use of the club house. Our committee would be delighted to worship at Harmony House for that price if you will permit it." Michael waited for the "sir", and when it came he welcomed them into the rest of the discussion. The food court was also available for their after-worship fellowship as long as the church custodian would manage the clean-up. The church organist, Sharon Krattz, (Which rhymes with fats, the reason for her anorexia,) would come by tomorrow afternoon to rehears.

As soon as he was dressed, Caleb was at his piano, going over melodies that might be appropriate for the church service. He was spot on for 80% of his choices. The twins joined him and together they filled the afternoon with delightful music.

Noell called Cheryl to tell her that there would be an unusual number of folks at Harmony House on Saturday. It would be an opportunity for an unexpected introduction to the Deli. As it turned out she was open at 9:00 o'clock and sold out by 2:00, more than four times a typical day. The fun part of that were the several folks who worked in the Aloha offices nearby who promised to bring their colleagues for lunch during the week. The church emergency was becoming a windfall reveal for the Deli. There was a rumor that Rusty had fourths of the Snicker Doodles.

The Lady's Guild showed up with a ten foot free-standing old rugged cross that stood behind the large folding table that had a lovely white cover. The satin material had a purple outline of a cross and was large enough to be adorned with three or four dozen Easter lilies. It was an attractive worship center. For Caleb and the twins the interesting part of the preparations began when Carrey James called to ask them to meet her and Miss Krattz, her piano teacher. They had an idea that would include them all in the Easter worship. She also told them that the paper had printed an invitation for the 10:00 o'clock Easter worship with the Aloha Christian church which was meeting at the Harmony House. "Attendance might be extra big even for an Easter."

As the trio walked into the auditorium Cam whispered, "It feels like we are visitors and they live here." Carrey and Miss Krattz were already seated at the grand piano.

"I'm happy to meet you in person," the teacher said. "Carrey talks about her best friends all the time. I was here for the piano party and think this auditorium is the very best idea ever." Her wide smile helped them overlook her dreadful gaunt frame.

Carrey said brightly, "Miss Krattz has offered us the prelude; you know, the music before the service begins. Do you remember at the piano party I played Handel's triumphant march from Judas Maccabeus, *'Thine Be the Glory'*?" She looked at Cele and Cam, "If you guys can learn it this evening, we can play four hands on the piano. Want to give it a try?" She had a delightful smile and extra copies of the music. Miss Krattz was getting a chair so she could comfortably watch.

The twin violins sang a simple nine note tuning cord before their first attempt at the music. Miss Krattz asked, "Is there a purpose to that little beginning?"

Cam answered brightly, "I'm tuned to the piano, and Cele is tuned to me. It is most important for us to be just the same."

Their first couple attempts were interrupted with giggles and apologies. Actually it only took a few minutes before piano and violins were singing beautifully together. The violins sang their brief tuning chord and were placed in their cases. Cam said that now that they had the melody and rhythm, they would go home and get really comfortable with the song. When Miss Krattz asked if they needed a ride home, Cele giggled, "Yes we do. We ride the elevator."

That was a puzzle to the teacher, but a greater puzzle was the hunger she was feeling for some delightful food. How long had it been since she had felt that? Years! She would think about this for a while, but she was certain her doctor would like to know that an appetite has returned. It was a day of happy surprises.

At the dinner table Caleb brought up a subject that he and Carrey had briefly talked about. "Dad, why don't we like the church?" His innocent expression suggested that this was an honest question.

"What makes you think we don't like it, son?" the dad asked in response.

"Well, if we liked it we would go, at least some of the time. I've never gone. Have you? If we don't go, it just stands to reason (he had heard his dad use that phrase often) that we don't like it." It was a fairly circular logic.

"I'm not sure that is the only reason folks don't go," Michael said softly. "Maybe it's like swimming. To learn to swim you need someone who will take you there and teach you how to hold your breath and paddle. Do you agree?" Caleb and the twins nodded. "I didn't have anyone who could take me to church when I was little and when I got big, I was learning how to be a soldier. Would you like to learn about the church?" Three children nodded in unison.

"Well I can't imagine a better opportunity than what is coming tomorrow. Like Grandma Helen said, 'If we won't go to church, maybe the church will come to us.'"

Caleb was the first one up and dressed. He began playing church hymns loud enough to awaken the rest of the house. By 7:30 they had all enjoyed Helen's Peanut Butter and Jelly French Toast. Since they were only waiting, the twins joined the Sunday morning serenade, becoming even more familiar with the selected hymns for the service. Finally at 9:00 o'clock they went down to the auditorium to wait for Miss Krattz and Carrey. Noell had a satisfied mom's smile at their anticipation.

When Cam explained that the violins could play the hymns, the teacher was understandably guarded. But when she heard them play there was no doubt about it. They would add volume and harmony to the piano. She was also delighted again to hear their nine note tuning chord.

The auditorium was just about full, even the balcony, when Carrey and Caleb made their way to the piano bench. The twins joined them and played a tuning chord. "*Thine Be the Glory*" began strong and concluded triumphant. As a young man welcomed the full house and thanked Harmony House for their gracious use of this place, the children traded places with Miss Krattz. There was a brief prayer and Miss Krattz invited the violins to join her. She gave them a tuning note and they replied with their chord, again so everyone could hear it. Sitting near the front on the side aisle near the piano an elderly lady dressed in a black coat smiled at their competence. The audience stood and sang *"Crown Him with Many Crowns."*

A high school girl went to the microphone and read Matthew 28: 1 – 6: "After the Sabbath, at dawn on the first day of the week, Mary Magdalene and the other Mary went to look at the tomb. There was a terrible earthquake for an angel of the Lord came down from heaven, and going to the tomb rolled back the stone and sat on it. His appearance was like lightning, and his clothes were white as snow. The guards were so afraid of him that they shook and became like dead men. The angel said to the women, 'Do not be afraid, for I know that you are looking for Jesus, who was crucified. He is not here. He has risen just as he said. Come and see the place where he lay. Then go quickly and tell the disciples: He has risen from the dead and is going ahead of you into Galilee. There you will see him."

Once again the audience sang an Easter hymn, *"Up from the Grave He Arose."*

That was followed by an Easter prayer before the choir sang: *"Easter People Raise Your Voices."* It was time for Pastor Carlson.

"When I look around at all these smiling faces and hear the glorious music, I believe we are receiving the manifestation of Easter. From the shock of last Friday's fire, the destruction of our treasured sanctuary to the gracious hospitality of caring friends and the joy of this morning we are receiving an Easter blessing. In the invocation you heard the words of Paul to the Colossians. 'God has given a vision of the full wonder and splendor of his secret plan for the sons of man. And the secret is simply this: 'Christ in you! Yes! Christ in you bringing with him hope of all the glorious things to come.' Could we have imagined last Friday morning that we would be in this place, with all of you, in Christ? It is a wonderful Easter image!

"Many of you will recall Dr. Sperling from the Fuller Institute that was with us five years ago. She gave us a tool that I have been using ever since. Almost every day my morning ritual has included a word to myself. I speak it out loud or I simply hear the words in my awareness. Sometimes I make it into a litany, repeating it over and over calming a tense moment or helping me focus on a nagging problem. 'Don, the secret is simply this: 'Christ in you! Yes! Christ in you brining with him the hope of all the glorious things to come."

"'In Christ,' was a recurring theme for Paul, the great apostle of Jesus and writer of this letter to the Colossians. In fact, his understanding of the Christian life revolved around two basic concepts. One, justification by faith, being made right with God, and two, being a person in Christ. Believing that the cross is the sign of God's amazing love for us is the faith of the first one. Living the Christian life means being in Christ. These were the well-spring of the flow of the Christian experience. Since it is an experiential concept, let me tell you about someone who embodied it for me.

"She was an attractive woman; perhaps in her early thirty's. She came into my study smiling, a sparkle in her eyes. This was not the same person with whom I had been counseling. Something had happened. She had changed.

"I had not seen her for three or four months, but prior to that she had been a regular. I remember the first time I met her. She showed up at our church one day, asking to see the counselor. None of us knew her. I'm glad I was available. I had never seen a more anxious, uncertain, nervous person. She slumped in the chair, glancing at me only occasionally, unconsciously clenching and opening her hands. She spoke haltingly, in jerky phrases, but managed to tell me amid the wreckage of jobs and relationships she had heard of our church's mission emphasis, particularly our work in Haiti. She was a nurse and wanted to share in that mission. If she couldn't be part of a visitation team, she'd like to contribute monthly in a financial way. The amount mentioned seemed excessive in light of her personal problems.

"That was the beginning of sporadic visits at first and then more regular ones, which were laced with guilt, fear, frustration at not being able to do more, or try harder to be the person she was supposed to be. Her conclusion was often to give more, do more, try harder. Her feelings were a need to prove herself, to earn respect, to be worthy of God's love.

"Those sessions left me feeling depressed, or at least frustrated that I couldn't be more helpful to her. That same feeling must have been hers as well, because one day she finally admitted that there were opposing forces working within her. 'One is happy and free,' she said with a thin smile. The other is fierce and restricted. It frightens me.' She sat hunched over, clenching and opening her hands symbolizing the struggle of a timid uncertain person.

"I told her of the old Native American saying that in everyone there are two wolves battling for survival. One is a bad wolf that is selfish and cruel; the other is gentle and gracious, a joy to others.

"Which one will win?" she asked timidly.

"The one you feed," I told her. "The bad wolf feeds on fear, envy, guilt, while the good wolf feeds on love, joy and peace.

"But I have no food for the good wolf," she moaned.

"That's not true," I counseled. God has loved you from your first breath. In Christ God has always loved you. There is nothing you can do to cause him to love you less, nor cause him to love you more. In Christ you have been a joy to your family and friends. In Christ you are a healing nurse bringing health and hope to others. The choice of which wolf to feed is yours."

She left my study that day in deep thought and I didn't see her for several weeks. She apparently went home to validate my counsel with her priest. She was amazed. Then she spent a weekend with her sister confirming the growing new awareness. Finally she went home and had a spirit-lifting conversation with her parents. It had been her perceptions and presumptions that had started her down a hurtful journey of trying to earn their affection. Eventually that fact got through to her and changed her life. She realized that with all her heart she wanted to be in Christ. Finally she came back into my study to thank me and tell me that she was scheduled to be with the Doctors Without Borders mission to Guatemala. Her smile was pleased and confident.

"Who is this person?" I thought to myself. "Certainly not the timid struggling, fear-filled person from before."

She used a marvelous symbol to explain her experience. "I was trying to pry open the window to get in the house when all the time the door was open, and I had only to walk in." That's an Easter experience.

Doesn't that sound like the words from Revelation 3? 'Behold, I stand at the door and knock; if anyone hears my voice and opens the door, I will come in to him and eat with him and he with me.'

Now there are many scholarly discussions about Easter. But none of them are more dramatic than the powerful change in the ones who saw it first. The women approached the tomb with a burden of oils to complete the burial of Jesus. They were in grief but moments later in his presence they were in Christ and their joy was unshakable. They ran to tell the disciples the victorious news. Simon Peter was in shame after the crucifixion. He had denied Jesus three times. In the Lord's presence he was forgiven in Christ and became the rock upon which the church was founded. Thomas was in doubt before Jesus appeared to them. The Lord invited those doubts to touch the wounds and in Christ, Thomas could only confess, 'My Lord and my God!' Saul of Tarsus was in angry opposition, hunting the early believers of Jesus to imprison them. When on the road to Damascus he met the risen Jesus. It was an Easter experience because in Christ he became the tireless missionary and writer of most of our New Testament.

This morning is powerful Easter! I wonder what you are in. I know that some of you are in pain, others are in grief or sorrow. You may be in boredom or confusion or frustration or guilt. You may be in doubt or disbelief. The good news of this day is that you need not remain there. Christ is alive and present with us, eager to give you a new beginning a fresh start. In Christ you may become a new person. Behold I stand at the door and knock, if anyone hears my voice and opens the door, I will come in to him and eat with him and he with me.'

"Perhaps you've already heard the recent story about the successful businessman who had a son that joined the military. In the desert of Iraq that son lost his life and the grief of that loss was too much for his mother's heart. She passed away leaving the businessman heartbroken and alone. The businessman had accumulated a marvelous art collection and when the pain of grief became too much for him too, he passed away. In the settlement of his estate, all that lovely art and his extensive estate were to be auctioned off. Bidders came from far and wide, eager for a chance to acquire a portion of prominence.

"The first item to be auctioned was a portrait of his son. The quality of the artist was only average and there was very little interest in that particular item. The auctioneer lowered the opening bid, and then lowered it again. Finally, the businessman's secretary offered a bid out of sheer sentiment. With no other bidders the auctioneer's hammer confirmed the sale and the auctioneer announced that the sale was over. On the back of the son's portrait was a note that said simply, 'Whoever takes my son gets everything.'

"Glorious Easter tells us that God loves us absolutely and unconditionally. God has a design for your life and the gifts to accomplish it. The first step is to receive his Son Jesus, the Risen Christ. Behold I stand at the door and knock; if anyone hears my voice and opens the door, I will come in to him and eat with him and he with me.' Let us pray."

Caleb felt the pastor's prayer was too long. It dulled the good feelings the sermon had given him. While Miss Krattz played a quiet song as the offering plates were passed around, he tried to recall the sermon and the important parts that he especially wanted to remember. Then the audience was invited to stand and sing the hymn *"He Lives!"* As he sang the last words of the refrain, "You ask me how I know he lives? He lives within my heart." Caleb found Carrey looking at him with a shy happy smile. Neither of them looked away for a long moment. There was ever so much to remember from this worship time, but that look was the happiest.

The announcements informed the folks that a fellowship opportunity of coffee and cookies was offered by the ladies of the church in the food court upstairs from the foyer and next Sunday's worship service would once again be here at Harmony House.

The food court was pretty well filled, some folks enjoying the tables and many more standing in groups. Ed and Helen wanted to introduce themselves as visitors from Minnesota. So they wandered from group to group. "Yes sir, Ed said for the twenty third time, "those three are our grandkids. Aren't they great?"

Near the corner, a group of music students seemed clustered around Caleb, Cele and Cam. Carrey was saying, "When you began, I almost croaked. You were more aggressive than we rehearsed. But when I followed you and Cele and Cam came in just as strong, it was wonderful." Her cheeks had a rosy flush proving her excitement.

Caleb said, "I hope Miss Krattz will ask us to help again." He was thinking this morning had been as much fun as his birthday.

With that shy smile, Carrey said, "She said that she would call me with the hymns just as soon as the pastor chooses them, but no later than Thursday. That should give us time to get to know them."

Cam had been watching Caleb. She didn't want to interrupt, but finally she asked, "Before we started our tuning chord, you were playing what sounded like church bells, and they were right on pitch for our first note. How did you know that?" Before he could answer she added, "And at the end when we were playing the chord again, the chimes were right with us. It made it feel so planned instead of just an accident. Will you do it all the time?"

Their brother just shrugged and said, "Only if you want me to."

Standing right next to them, but not part of their conversation, Kenny was telling Michael and Rusty James about the mysterious paper that turned to powder. "Dr. Wayne Sheldon, Cheryl's dad was fascinated. He's a Chemistry Professor at Portland State and had heard about the process but had never seen it. I think those clips we captured are going viral. He said that near the end of the sixteenth century, covert communication was just getting a beginning, mostly with invisible ink that reacted to heat or certain fluids. In 1700 there was a William Rittenhouse who relocated his paper mill from Krefeld Germany to Pittsburg. The cause for his immigration was religious persecution in the region we now think of as the Netherlands. He was a Mennonite, which meant as a pacifist he would flee rather than fight. He developed something called 'Candle Paper.' It seems he experimented, using Hydrogen Peroxide instead of water in his pulp mixture. The paper was much thinner than ordinary paper and very white. The amazing side of it was that until it was warmed by sunlight it was quite stable But the photosensitive reaction allowed the hydrogen to return to a gas form, leaving only powder dry pulp. What we saw in the box is simply dried paper pulp. There is nothing extraordinary or secret about it. But he does think there will be a lot of interest in paper-makers today to develop a product like it that will more quickly break down in recycling. You may hear from some to have permission to use the stuff we salvaged."

Rusty started to say something and Kenny asked for one last item. "Michael, you will be contacted by a Dr. Sarah Laven. She's trying to translate our photos. 'Scuse me Rusty. You were going to ask a question."

"Yeah," Rusty said with a grin. "You guys seem pretty tight with each other. Have you worked on other projects or something?"

Michael answered for them. "Nope. About a year and a half ago Kenny's construction company was building this for the Koreans. A zoning code could not be modified and they went bankrupt. I was able to pick it up and changed it into an auditorium and a very comfortable living space. For about nineteen months he has put up with my grouchy shortsightedness."

Karen, Rusty's wife asked, "Are you saying that your residence is part of this building? I had no idea."

Noell got into the conversation by adding, "Kenny's architect was genius in helping me with the layout and design. If you can wait a while for the crowd to thin, we would love to show it to you. I'm just not comfortable with an unplanned open house."

Cheryl added, "They have let me start a part-time deli ." She pointed to the sign. "We're doing more business than I imagined possible. And don't believe Michael. He is never grouchy if he has a Snicker Doodle."

Rusty asked softly as though those nearby might be listening, "Do you think that architect might take a look at a hundred year old sanctuary and give us some ideas about repairing the fire damage. Since there was a lot of damage, we might have an opportunity to remodel the old girl."

Noell smiled and thought to herself. "We planned this wonderful building for the children. Today I have four new friends who feel so much like family I am eager to welcome them into our home." She looked at Michael and wished that she could show him how very precious he was to her. Her smile grew as she knew that she would do that later.

The first day of school after a week of vacation is always testy. Getting back in the routine is a challenge. Cele and Cam were going into the restroom to wash their hands before lunch when two frightened girls rushed out. As the twins stepped into the room they saw Carrey James sitting on the floor holding her face that had an angry pink hand mark. She was crying because she had been slapped by a large sixth grade bully. Two more girls hurried out of the back stalls, taking advantage of the momentary interruption.

Cam asked in a shocked voice, "What are you doing to our sister?"

Virginia Matson, the largest girl in the school turned toward them and growled, "This is none of your business unless you want to get popped too." She took a menacing half step toward the two.

Curiously, Cam didn't say anything, but hummed a steady note. Instructions were filling her mind giving her a plan. Cele glanced at her and then joined with the first note of their tuning chord. Virginia's scowl turned into a grimace of curiosity as she leaned to finish that step toward them. Quickly nine notes were hummed and

Cam said in a commanding voice the words that were flooding her mind, "As still as a stump!"

Virginia didn't take another step but stood perfectly still. The room was silent.

The twins stepped around the larger girl and helped Carrey to her feet. As she hugged the two, Cam encouraged her to come with them but hesitated before hurrying out. "That's strange," she murmured because the words continued. "I would never have thought to do that," she said with a half smile. She asked Cele for a marking pen. Very carefully she printed "BULLY" on Virginia's forehead. There was no movement of resistance from the girl who stood as still as a stump. Before she hurried out, Cam whispered softly to Virginia, "If you harm another child, I will turn you into a stone statue forever." At the door, she hummed a single note until Cele joined her. They quickly went through the nine note chord and closed the door.

Virginia looked around the empty bathroom trying to recall why she had come in. She hurried to lunch surprised by the strange stares she received on the way. It would turn out to be a very puzzling afternoon for her.

Carrey clung to Cam on the way to the cafeteria. There were only a couple sobs that escaped. She kept muttering, "Thank you. I don't know what just happened. I've never been hit. It was like a bad dream until you came in and rescued me. What just happened?" Another little sob shook her.

When Virginia arrived at the cafeteria there were enough looks and snickers to cause her to peer into a reflection on the coke machine. It took her a moment to understand the word written on her forehead. In a burst of anger she exploded. "If I catch whoever did this I'll…" Suddenly a danger signal went off in her memory and she imagined herself as a stone statue. She began rubbing the word until a teacher suggested that she go to the nurse's office, where they could use some rubbing alcohol to remove it.

On the far side of the lunchroom, Carrey was holding her milk carton against her cheek. The cold application had chased away the sting and most of the pink handprint. "I don't know what you did," she said quietly. "But I do remember that you called me your sister. That was wonderful."

On their way to their afternoon class, Cam whispered to Cele, "Let's not tell Caleb about that, O.K.?" When there was an agreeing nod she added, "But I'll tell daddy, when I get a chance. I always want to be true to him."

The Wednesday morning breakfast was a bit subdued. Ed and Helen had to say goodbye to their grandchildren, but they promised it would be only for a while. Ed promised that they would return soon. "If you will let us visit again we were thinking of spending Christmas with you," Ed said hopefully. Noell had noticed the absence of any petulant or abrasive comments from him recently.

Helen added softly, "I know it is very presumptuous of us, so please forgive this suggestion. Noell, neither of your brothers are married and we haven't seen either of them for five or six ears. Ritchie is in Florida and Paul is in Iraq. Maybe they would come here if you invited them. We have so missed them since they got out of school. They might be inspired, just as we have been, to be in this amazing place with you amazing people." Her gaze embraced the family of five at the table. Her shy smile underscored a Christmas hope.

Michael joined the conversation by asking, "Do I recall that Paul is in the Navy? What's a sailor doing in all that sand?"

Ed answered proudly, "He's a Hospital Corpsman first class with the Marine Corps brigade there."

A warm smile bloomed on Michael's face. "If you'll give me the contact information, I will personally invite him. I'll bet the men of the brigade call him "Doc". That's pretty standard. I'd really like to meet him and we have lots of room."

On Thursday afternoon, Mr. Klein called Michael's cell phone to inform him that a rather surly man who claims to represent the department of licensing was at the front door, requesting to speak to the school director. "He seems rather concerned about our ability to continue operations at Harmony House."

As Michael came out the front door, the well dressed man seemed to be evaluating the building and shaking his head. "This isn't right," Michael heard him say.

When Michael introduced himself as the Director of Harmony House and held out his hand, the man continued to shake his head, but not Michael's hand.

"Oh, there are several violations I can see from here," the man said. "But the ones that need immediate correction is your operating a school without a city permit, a church without a city permit, and an underground parking facility, again with no permit. Without immediate payment, it is my unpleasant duty to demand a cease and desist order. I must shut you down."

Michael had seen some lame hustles, but this one took the cake for unbelievable. "Damn, what can I do about that? We have students coming for classes and Sunday morning there will be hundreds of folks disappointed if you shut us down. What can we do about this?" he asked again and looked very distraught.

"Well, you can write a check today or go down to the city office next week and try to get a council hearing. But without a permit, you cannot continue. Maybe you just want to shut it down for a few days," the man huffed.

"Oh no, we can't do that we have tried so hard to get it going. That would ruin everything. How much is a permit?" Michael was trying to seem desperate.

The man looked at the sheet of paper on his clipboard. "Let's see. The permit for the school is $750 and the permit for the church is just the same. The underground parking is only $500," he concluded with satisfaction.

"Can we make a partial payment now and do the rest in installments?" asked the one who seemed in real distress.

"No," the man said a bit testy. "I told you that you must have a permit to continue. I can take a check or a credit card."

"Well may I see some identification at least?" Michael said sounding close to tears.

The man turned the clip board toward him and pointed to the letterhead. It seemed authentic city of Aloha stationary, or a close facsimile.

"You know, that looks pretty convincing. It's your identification I asked for, however," Michael said a bit whiney.

The man shrugged and answered, "I'm just a collector doing my job. I'll shut you down if you insist."

Michael asked, "Is that Glock 9 on your hip part of your collection protection?" His voice was no longer timid or passive.

When the man took a step backwards, Michael said, "You can sit down while I call the police, or I'll help you down." He took a step toward the man who now understood there would be no permit payment. In desperation, the man made the mistake of reaching for the gun. It came out of the holster as Michael's vice-like grip held the man's hand. There was a tiny bit of struggling as awareness set in that this mark was no pansy. Just as he was about to scream, "don't hurt me!" the gun pointed down at the ground and went off. The bullet went through the top of the man's foot and he screamed in pain, released the gun from his hand into Michael's and fell to the ground.

"As I said, 'I'll help you down.' Now stay there or I will really hurt you."

The police were there in only a few minutes. Mr. Klein had witnessed the incident and the security camera had captured every moment of it. The phony document on Aloha letterhead was convincing and proof of the struggle for the gun before he shot himself in the foot was all the additional evidence needed. The con man had a lengthy history of theft and extortion. There was little for the officers to do but put him in the aid car and file new arrest papers. One of the officers asked what time the church service would be on Sunday.

For Michael the most regrettable part of the incident was his rush of adrenalin and the jolt of satisfaction in the physical combat, albeit brief. He wasn't sure how he would explain this to Noell, or manage the urge to be back in active duty.

Dinner was over. Her mom was busy in the kitchen, Caleb was in the music room playing the piano, Cele was in her room playing the hymns for Sunday and her dad was reading a magazine in the media room. Cam sat down beside him and began, "I learned something scary." Her dad gave his full attention and she continued, "We went in the washroom and a bully girl had banged Carrey James down for no reason. Virginia turned on us and threatened to bang Cele and me and I had words like instructions in my head. I think our violins were helping us because I hummed the beginning of our violin chord. Cele joined with me and the big girl stood still, sort of like she was asleep. I told her to stand as still as a stump and she did." Michael's expression was pure concern.

"We helped Carrey up, but before we left the restroom I told Virginia if she ever hurt another child I would turn her into a stone statue and I printed 'Bully' on her forehead with a marking pen. She didn't move at all. We went to the door and hummed the chord again and ran. We saw her in the cafeteria but she didn't pay any attention to us. Do you think I should tell Miss Ross what I did? I only wanted to help Carrey." Cam was still awaiting the verdict.

Michael repeated her account with a slight smile, "and you didn't touch or hurt her in any way?"

"Well I did write on her. She just stood as still as a stump," Cam shrugged. The half smile she wore was evidence that she didn't feel in trouble, more like she was in a puzzle.

Her dad asked for more information. "What made you think about humming? Most girls would be screaming as they ran in circles. Didn't you think about running away?"

She shook her curls. "Daddy, we had to help Carrey. The print on her face was from a hard slap. We had to do something. My violin told me what to do and what to say. It was like she was inside my head."

"But you could have helped Carrey by finding a teacher," the dad said still looking for the answer of an interesting riddle.

She nodded in agreement. "I could have but I didn't need a teacher. It was like my violin was telling me what to do and Cele understood right away how to help. No one was hurt and Carrey likes us even more." Now the smile bloomed into something Michael recognized. She was feeling satisfaction after a positive resolution of conflict, sort of the way he felt after the bogus con man was arrested.

He pulled her over closer to him so he could kiss the top of her head. "I'm proud of you two. You were brave in helping your friend. But I think this should be a secret between us right now. I'm not sure if your mom would approve."

"Well, she sort of knows part of the secret because she was there when Mrs. Gleason said that we could protect the violins and they had the power to protect us." She sat back so she could look into his deep brown eyes. "But I think it is best we don't tell her. You know she gets worried about every little thing." She was happy to have told him and happier that they had a secret.

In the comfort of darkness and their cozy bed, Noell pressed herself spooning against Michael. She pulled his arm more tightly around her and shivered with the comfort. Several moments passed before she asked quietly, "Do you ever think about your old life?" Before he could answer, she asked, "Do you miss the Corps and wish you had some exciting assignment on the other side of the world?"

He tightened his hold on her and asked, "Why would you ever think such a thing, especial when we are like this?"

"I know it has only been two years, but I think I understand you. You shot a guy and bundled him off to the police. I'll bet that got your blood racing. You know, old habits are hard to break."

In the stillness and closeness he marveled at her insight and wondered how he could love her more. "You know, the funny thing about that was I did get a rush from that little scuffle. And to be perfectly clear, he shot himself."

She snorted, "With your accurate help."

Michael continued, "I did have a momentary thought about the assignments and the brotherhood of team mates. But my first thought was about you; there was no true satisfaction with those missions. I have never been as fulfilled as I am here with you and the kids." His arm tightened just a bit more and she knew that words were no longer necessary.

The breakfast dishes were cleared and the children off to school when the phone rang. "Good morning Mr. Winter, I'm Sarah Laven from Portland State U Language Department. A few weeks ago Kenny Fox brought me some prints of a fascinating bit of history you folks discovered."

"I'm glad to hear from you Dr. Laven. I've been curious to learn about that hidden cache."

"I can imagine you would be with paper that self-disintegrates obliterating writing that is in an extremely old language. Are you interested?"

"That's the understatement of the morning. I can't imagine what value that information might have years and years after it was left here, but yes, I am interested." Michael's voice was warm and friendly.

"Not years and years, but centuries; do you have time this afternoon to stop by my office and talk about it? I'll tell you that it has been a challenge to interpret, but a very satisfying one. My last class is over by two. I usually leave by five."

Michael asked if Kenny Fox could accompany him and the plans were set. When he called Kenny he was told that the contractor was eager for an Intermission Deli lunch and would happily accompany Michael to Portland U after they had Snicker Doodles.

He was expecting a dumpy middle-aged large woman but Dr. Sarah Laven was none of those. The woman who shook hands with them was petite and graceful, like a dancer. She smiled warmly and thanked them for a spring-break distraction. When Michael slid the check across her desk saying that he hoped this might be compensation for her hours of translation, her smile grew wider and she exclaimed that it was wonderfully generous. "With this I can get new skies in the fall and perhaps make the national team after all. I broke my slalom boards last month. This will be a great upgrade. I might even get a sponsor." Her little giggle was pure gratitude. Michael and Kenny were seated on the other side of her desk.

"Well gentlemen, where shall we begin?" she said brightly. "First, this was a copy, a very poor copy, of several other documents. I got the feeling the author was trying to glean a whole library into a few pages. I counted twenty seven pages written in at least four different languages. It began with Low German, which means neither formal nor proper. The spelling was terrible and my feeling was that the writer didn't understand the material he or she was copying. Next was Croatian which we would call street linguistics, which again had tons of errors. There followed a large portion written in Netherland Dutch, probably the scribe's native language. The references of that part spoke of heart breaking oppression. The latter documents were a partial record of their efforts to find an American place where they could have a fresh start. Amazingly, I found the name of Jeremy Gottschalk of North Newton, Kansas, who happened to be my great great grandfather." There was a tear in her eyes. "There are hundreds of names of pioneer settlers. He just happened to be one who was seeking religious freedom as well."

Her voice became more like a lecturer. "Now for the content, there are at least four parts that sort of dovetail together. The first part seemed to be a record of victims of persecution. There were several pages lost before you began to capture them. This material seems to be from a book entitled *Martyrs' Mirror*. It graphically tells about the Catholic Church's attempts to maintain orthodoxy by power. For example there was an account from 1569 of a man named Dirk Willems who was making a run for it. As a pacifist he could not resist so flight was his only choice. He went around the frozen lake and the man following him tried a short cut. The ice was not strong enough to support him and he crashed through. Dirk could have escaped but because he had seen the emergency, he scooted out and rescued his pursuer who promptly arrested him anyway. Dirk Willems was burned at the stake.

"This section also has the account of a priest named Menno Simons who was aware of the activity of Martin Luther. In the year 1536 Menno left the priesthood and began a separate ministry. You saved the seven articles he wrote, apparently for the instruction or direction of small fellowships to follow. They were:

"The ban, which is a shorter word than excommunication or shunning but was the most common form of this practice. I can't imagine how a person would feel if they were completely ignored by friends and family, as though they weren't even there.

Breaking Bread, seen as a sacrament in the Catholic Church, is here called a memorial of the last supper and the concept of transubstantiation is rejected.

This new fellowship is a separation from the Catholic Church and not to be seen as an additional part of it.

Baptism is an adult sign of faith in the One God. It is for adults only.

Sexuality is a gift from God expressly for procreation. Chastity in singleness and fidelity in marriage are the only faithful expressions of that. A pastor is ordained or designated by the elders to maintain the sanctity of those conditions.

The fellowship shall renounce the sword by practicing pacifism.

The fellowship shall renounce every oath except that to God. Swearing as proof of the truth is an infringement."

"I got too sleepy reading all of the fine print of theology, but I'm pretty sure I covered the main issues." Michael liked Dr. Laven's attitude a lot. He thought he would probably get sleepy reading those points too.

"There are two other parts that I believe are connected, but they are in different languages. There is a Low German story from the 14th century of a vagabond named Till Eulenspiegel who is sometimes called a trickster or a prankster. His name means 'Owl–Glass'. Usually his practical jokes confuse a laborer or exasperate a cook. Someone was tricked into exposing her vices or his greed or hypocrisy. There is considerable poetry and songs about him for he is a happy vagrant and a considerable trouble-maker. Usually he complicates conversations by using words improperly. Most of the images we have of jesters are depictions of Till Eulenspiegel.

"The development of that character, however, changed as the persecution increased. His name was retranslated to mean Owl-Mirror, a reference to the martyrs. By the middle of the 16th century Till characters, usually hired by the priest to disrupt protestant worship, were disrupting services and doing things that were disgusting and inappropriate. The term 'scatological' came from their soiling the sanctuary, even depositing feces on the alter calling it the waste of Christ. One account tells of the prankster interrupting the morning by shaking the priest's hand before the service with a hand covered with feces. Yes disruptive for sure. The custom of Menno Simons' was to bolt the church doors closed from the inside during the service to keep out those who would try to be disrespectful."

Sarah took a deep breath and said, "The lecture is nearly over, fellows. The next part of my translation came from a friend who works in immigration. She identified the account as Croatian from early in the 17th century. Stoel the Gypsy was a violin maker of exceptional skill with his twin brother Loets. Remember that was sixty years before the Italian Antonio Stradivari was making his. This account is a careful description of their use of mountain Spruce that is very dense for the frame and neck of two instruments. Straight grain Willow from the land of a royal was used for the lining and Maple from a sunny climate was used for the top and bottom of the violins. They made sure the instruments were exact, except for their color. One was white as snow; the other had the color of royalty. Finally a circle of five priestesses touched the instruments and prayed that they might be ageless as they chase away evil and bring healing and comfort to the injured. If the violins would ever be separated they would only bring sorrow.

"In the year 1630 Reigner the soldier and Ilsa his wife had twin girls. He wanted to name them Valr, which means battlefield and Kjose, to choose. Together they would be Wala and Kuzjon, the Valkyrje. They would choose who on the battlefield survived and who did not. One of them would escort the spirit of the fallen warrior to Valhalla to live with Odin. When not in battle mode they would be lovers of heroes and carry mead to the thirsty warriors.

"In the year 1666 there must have been something catastrophic because Ilsa and Kjose are in the Netherlands with the violins. They find a Norse couple, Helgi and Segran who have five year old twin daughters. Curiously they have named their daughters Oskmey (May for short), which means 'wish maid', and 'Oski' (Key" for short), which means 'wish filler' and the legacy continues."

"The final entry in the ledger is written in Dutch; it is dated1731. Key, who is alone, has found a sea captain named van Mills and his wife Ursula who have infant daughters. There are no names given of the girls and only the hope that the violins will continue to thrive in their new land.

"On the last page given to me there is a collection of travel journals of a small group of pioneers. 1809 is in the margin and Lydia Krounse has the violins in Pennsylvania. Apparently they could find no favorable homestead so the group continued to the Ohio territory where they are joined by another band of Mennonites. In Kansas Muriel and Millicent Neufeld are twins who become keepers of the violins in 1843 as they continue west.

"The last accounts are those of the group's challenges with Till Eulenspiegel. In Utah, and Idaho they have a rolling skirmish, apparently encounters with both natives and ranchers who harass them repeatedly. The final line says that in the year 1881 they are entering the Oregon territory and can go no further west. If the violins cannot save them they will disband and seek shelter in anonymity. It is signed, 'In Amity.'"

Dr. Laven shook her head as though clearing her thoughts. "Thank you for this opportunity. I felt as though I was a part of their story for a while. Do you know anything more about these people or whatever happened to the violins? I suspect if they still exist they are worth a fortune." She pushed the pile of pages across to Michael.

He shook his head too, saying, "This is all we know since we found a box under a pile of rocks on the Aloha property. Thank you for allowing us to touch this thread of history." He stood up; apparently it was time to go. Kenny shook her hand and as Michael did too he said, "You might come and visit us some Sunday at Harmony House. Our twins love to meet guests." He gave her a business card.

Her raised eyebrow and tilted head suggested surprise and curiosity. He was pretty sure they would see one another again.

As they pulled in the Hospitality House driveway, Michael noticed Pastor Carlson waiting in the foyer. He waved and a moment later greeted them. "Noell told me you were on the way here so I just waited," he explained. "I hope you have a spare minute. My question really affects you both." He took a breath and smiling said, "The Trustees love the remodel proposal, especially since the insurance company is going to pay nearly half of it." Looking at Kenny he asked, "Do you still think it can be finished in two months?"

Kenny nodded, "I'm sure it can be useable in that time. There may be some of the trim work and stained glass that will take a little longer to get here. But it will be structurally sound."

Looking at Michael Pastor Don smiled and asked, "Do you think we might impose upon your generosity for eight more weeks? With the Trustees approval we will need a quick all-church meeting next Sunday. You have been very gracious. I think that was the best Easter congregation since I came here as pastor. May we continue to use this space?"

Michael answered, "I believe that is doable. The insurance company is probably picking up that cost as part of the settlement.

We will use that money to complete the percussion instruments for the youth symphony. They are preparing for a big inaugural show on Memorial Day."

The pastor had planned to ask for use of the food court for a couple meetings and choir rehearsal on Thursday evenings. Prudence wisely helped him be satisfied to have a lovely place to worship. They could get by with the limited undamaged space at the church.

Michael noticed the hesitation, so he asked, "Would the food court be large enough for your all-church meeting after fellowship time? I don't think it will be available often, but this is a pretty special occasion."

It must have been a day for questions because after supper Caleb found his dad in the office. "Dad, will you help me?" He had learned not to ask if he could ask a question. When his dad responded, "What's on your mind?" Caleb said, "You're a cool man. Will you tell me how to get a girlfriend?" He glanced around alert for eavesdroppers.

"Yeah, that's a pretty tough question. Can you tell me what you want her for? Will she play catch with you?" Caleb grimaced and shook his head. "Well then, do you want a girlfriend you can ask over for dinner and a movie?" Again Caleb shook his head. "Maybe you want a girlfriend who will dance with you and hold your hand."

Caleb once again rejected the idea by saying, "I'm only in the fourth grade."

"So you want someone who will like you, talk with you, be interested in the things you like to do, is that it?" Michael's smile was relaxed and so was Caleb's.

"Yup, I think that would be a good girlfriend," the lad replied.

Speaking in a hushed voice, Michael said softly, "Then here's a foolproof secret. Girls like guys who listen to them. They like guys who are smart but don't try to prove it all the time. Girls like to laugh, but not at someone's expense. If you want a girl to be interested in you, you have to be interesting. Girls like to know that you admire what they do. Does that sound like anyone you know?"

Caleb frowned as he tried to think of someone. "Nope, I can't think of anybody like that."

"Well pal, when you get a little smarter you will understand that a friend like Carrey James just fits that description. She is cute, sweet, and smart; she plays the piano almost as well as you do and she really likes you. All you will need to do is give her an honest compliment each day and listen a little better. You might also think what would cause her to want a boyfriend like you." He ruffled Caleb's hair and gave him a hug, satisfied with his fatherly advice.

Noell spent a lot of time writing letters to her brothers. They all had changed and it was like a stranger writing to another stranger. She apologized repeatedly and tried to convince them of her affection. Then she tore the letters into pieces and started over. She told them her life in Portland was marvelous now that she was married to a man who loved her and the kids and she really hoped it would be possible for them to enjoy their comfortable place here in Portland as they became reacquainted with one another. She gave them a brief introduction to their nephew and darling nieces. She closed by requesting a reply and sent them her affection.

It took ten days before she received reply from Ritchie. He thanked her for the reunion letter but he and his partner were already scheduled for a Hawaiian honeymoon. He promised to send pictures,

It took ten days for her letter to Paul to get to him. The Fleet Post Office forwarded the letter to the VA Navy Hospital in Baltimore. It took another two weeks for her to get his reply. He wrote: "Hi Sis, good to hear from you. The last letter I received said that you were hitching up with a big-time Hollywood producer. I'm glad to hear you have found someone who understands what a gem you are.

"I've learned that the military is hurry, hurry, hurry and then wait. I was in the backseat with Gabriel hurrying north of Bagdad when a roadside IED took out our vehicle. The driver and shotgun were killed. I lived because Gabe took most of the shrapnel. I think it was when the vehicle rolled on me that my back, hip and leg were broken. They shipped me here to Baltimore to get put back together again. Those injuries are service ending. Poor old Gabe is here too. Without an eye and part of his foot he was mustered out of the Corps with me. He's a four year old black German Shepherd bomb dog. I owe him my life.

"About Christmas, Sis, my long range plan right now is my next toilet visit. I'll be here at least a month or six weeks, then it will be a rehab station for another stretch. I remember how we used to make plans for our lives. I would sure welcome one of those chat sessions now. I've thought about getting a job as a trauma nurse. But I think my dream is to get to med school and become a trauma physician. Do you think it is too late to dream big dreams? Let's talk about it, what do you say? Thanks for the contact. You're it!"

Ten minutes after she read that letter to Michael she was on the phone calling the VA Navy Hospital in Baltimore. She was determined to tell him it is never too late. She is proof of that. At the same time Michael was calling Miss Krattz, offering a handsome gratuity for staying with the children for three days. Then he called American Airlines and booked two first class seats to Baltimore and made reservations at a hotel within walking distance of the hospital. His last task in this group was making contact with the veterinarian who was caring for Gabriel. They wanted to meet that courageous hero who had saved Paul's life.

Once again in the privacy of their room she leaned against him and asked, "How do I know that you love me? It was so evident today. When you heard the news about Pauly, you swung into action as though he was your brother. You've never met him but all of a sudden he is the focus of the morning. Thank you, Lover. You've just shown me another way to make love."

Baltimore was a combination of old buildings and crooked streets. "Wow, Michael, I thought LA was crowded." She was gazing at the eleven story hospital across a jammed street. "I thought west coast traffic was bad."

He chuckled, "When you think that this street existed before the California gold rush happened, it puts a different understanding on it." They crossed the street with a crowd and joined the line for the security guard at the VA hospital. Michael showed his ID and wrote the name of the person they were there to see. The security guard politely directed then to the information desk. It was so familiar to Michael, and yet like a lifetime ago. Eventually they were on the ninth floor, recovery, not sure what they were about to see. The door was ajar so they went in and found a man with his left leg in a cast that extended halfway up his torso. His eyes were closed, but when Noell turned to go back out the door, the patient said, "Come on in Sonny. I've been on pins and needles hoping you could find me." That nickname was a childhood conglomeration of Sweetie and Honey.

Noell turned quickly toward the name she had been called as a girl. The blue eyes and wide smile warmed her heart. "Hi Pauly. I've been walking on air knowing that I could see you." She rushed to the bedside and kissed his forehead. "Are you in much pain?"

"Naw, they are taking great care of me." He had wires and tubes connecting him to a quiet machine. "Who's the handsome hunk you brought with you? He sure doesn't look like a movie director."

"Pauly, this is Michael, the mighty angel I told you about."

Michael stepped near the bed and placing his hand on the available should said, "Semper fi, Doc." So began several minutes of fence-mending for lost time and bridge-building for a successful recovery. Michael was delighted to see Noell so bubbly. It was obvious that she adored her brother.

Eventually he told them that the spine fracture had been fused, the hip repaired with some screws and the femur fracture had been close enough to the knee to require a foam shield to the meniscus.

"That one will require the longest healing time," Paul reported. There was still a whole bunch of things to talk about when the nurse came in and announced that it was time to wind it down for today. In the farewell Michael said that they still had a stop to make at the Vet hospital to see Gabriel. They had been told again by Paul that he would not be alive for sure but for the strength of that dog. "If you get a chance to see him, ask if he wants a cookie, or call him 'Cookie Monster.' He loves that. I worry about the future disposition for him. We were both a big mess when I last saw him."

Noell kissed his cheek again and said, "We're staying just across the street so may we drop in again tomorrow afternoon?"

"Sure," her smiling brother said. "I'd invite you for lunch, but you would have to take it through a tube." It was great to see that his humor was intact and he had a clear understanding of his situation.

When Michael gave the taxi driver the Rosedale address of the veterinary Hospital the driver said, "That will be a $75 fare."

Michael responded, "We're only going to be there a few minutes. If you'll wait for us I'll make it an even $200 round trip."

"Yeah, I'm ready for a coffee break anyway," the driver said. "You folks must not be from around here. I'd guess Midwest. Most folks around here try to pinch the price down, not figure out a way to pay me more. Sit back and relax it will take about twenty five minutes in this traffic."

The receptionist said that the doctor was pretty busy. But when Michael explained the nature of their business the doctor came out immediately. He guided them into the back where there were several large crates. "Gabriel has been in considerable discomfort since the surgery to repair his wounds. We're waiting for the Navy to decide what to do with him. I think the lack of appetite is also a sign of his grief. The last he saw of his handler they were both in considerable distress and survival was not a given for either of them." They stopped in front of a crate where Gabriel lay, not even looking up. Much of his left side had been shaved, and Michael counted nine sutured surgery sites. The left ear was gone and the eye socket was empty. The side of his head and his left foot were heavily bandaged. The doctor said, "We haven't had instructions as to the amount or length of treatment for this dog. The nature and number of injuries means the service can't use him as broken as he is and he certainly could not be placed in a home with as much continuing care as that empty eye socket will need. It is our opinion that he should be put down."

Michael said softly, "Well I'm glad we stopped by this afternoon. We will take that option off the table for damned sure." Looking at the wounded Shepherd, he said, "Semper fi, Cookie Monster!" The big dog's head came up off the floor. "You want a cookie, pal?" Michael asked. He had stopped in the hospital cafeteria hoping for this opportunity. Looking at the vet, he asked "Will you open the door for a moment, I have a gift from Hospital Corpsman Paul Frost for his partner."

The vet started to explain that this patient was in no condition to.… Michael reached over and flipped the handle on the gate and opened the crate saying, "Doc Frost wants you to have a cookie, Pal. Semper fi." The big tail wagged a couple times and the open mouth accepted the offering. Michael closed the gate and said to the doctor, "This warrior earned a purple heart saving the only life he could in the explosion. There is no question about what you will do with him. You will help him pull it together. Corpsman Frost has a broken back, hip and leg. When he is ready to be released into rehab he will be living with us in Portland, not Maine but Oregon. As soon as this guy is ready for rehab, let me know and we will have him flown out there too." The words were said softly, but with intensity enough for the vet to understand that this was not a discussion. "Here's my card. If you send me an itemized statement I'll cover whatever the Navy doesn't. Does that sound doable?" When the vet nodded, Michael concluded, "Here's a few cookies for Gabe. With each one tell him, 'Doc Frost says, Get off your butt and get well.' Those two guys need each other to heal." Noell hadn't said a word, but let the happy tears that ran down her cheeks be her eloquent affirmation.

The vet held out his hand saying, "Thank you, Sir. Some of the time I forget that combat is real not just a lot of politicians playing footsy. We'll take good care of Gabriel and make sure that he gets cookies and our best care. We'll keep you apprised of his progress."

She was quiet for a few minutes as the taxi made their way back to the hotel. Finally she hooked her arm under his and said, "I just figured out why living with you is such a delight." When he looked into her blue eyes she continued, "You know what should be done and do it. We don't waste a lot of precious time worrying about details. I've been fretting about Pauly's recovery; you know, where will he live? How will he get the care he needs? How will he find a job or go to school? But you already know, don't you? You already have a plan that is the best. I have heard you say, 'It only takes the right people and enough resources to do the job right.' We have both!" She buried her face against his neck and whispered, "I love you, and have so much more to learn about that."

In the morning the City Tour sight-seeing bus picked them up in front of their hotel. Sunday morning traffic was light so their two hour tour had a bit more time to hear about the points of interest and their introduction to patriotic landmarks. While the historic significance of the area was important to Noell, her enthusiasm was definitely in anticipation of another visit with Pauly.

Once again his eyes were closed when she peaked into his room and once again he said without opening them, "Hi Sonny. You smell really nice." She hurried to his bedside to kiss him again. As before, Michael's warm smile expressed his satisfaction in seeing Noell so immersed in reestablishing her connection with her brother.

Eventually Paul was able to ask, "So, Michael, you were in the Corps?"

"I was," he answered gladly. "Thirteen years in NSA Special Forces, mostly in drug interdiction. It was pretty messy."

Paul's voice became more subdued as he asked, "How in the world did you meet Sonny," he corrected himself, "Noell? I can't imagine her in any way mixed up with drugs."

Noell answered for Michael. "No, Heinrik had hired a team of killers to get rid of me and the kids. Through an agency I was fortunate enough to hire Michael as security. He brought a couple of his team and took care of the problem, all of it."

"What did the authorities think about that?" Paul asked. "That sounds like a battlefield."

Noell quickly added, "And Phillip, Heinrik's brother, with four of his bodyguards kidnapped the kids in a conspiracy with the attorney. They were after the estate and needed me and the kids out of the way. Michael took care of them too."

Michael quickly interjected. "I, nor the others, were ever implicated. It was a righteous in and out. What do you say we talk about the future instead of the past? I think you will be glad to know that the Cookie Monster received a treat from you yesterday and encouragement to get with the program of healing. He's pretty dinged up, but now that he knows you're in recovery, he is too. Are you up for a suggestion?"

"That's good news about Gabriel. I hope he can find a good home." Paul's voice broke a bit just thinking about his furry big buddy.

"Oh he already has," Michael said quietly. "Some folks from Portland are going to take him in as soon as he can travel." His eyes held Paul's. "Those same folks are going to offer you a very comfortable place to finish your rehab as soon as you can travel. We thought he might be an inducement for you to come visit us for a while."

Noell scooped her arm around Michael's. "Pauly, we have tons of space and would be honored to help you get completely healed. Along the way you can decide what you want to do with the rest of your life. It's just the first step."

Michael said softly, "The President of the University of Oregon Med School in Portland is Dr. Titus Nichols. He welcomes a conversation with you as soon as you're patched up. He said a battle-trained nine year corpsman would be a delight in his program. You could receive credit for life experience. The students there do their internship at Legacy Good Samaritan Hospital, the largest and best trauma center in Oregon. That may be a second or third step. At least it's something to think about instead of that cute red headed nurse."

Tears were in Paul's eyes as he said, "Damn Michael! You were never implicated and you already have claim to Gabriel? You're the big brother I never had and Sonny got you for me." He held out his hand, not wanting to shake hands but hold his. "Semper Fi!" he said strongly.

Michael was convinced that the healing process was not going to take as long as the VA staff here predicted.

April slid by slowly. The twins had a pizza party with most of their third grade classmates in the food court. There was another trip to Baltimore. Both patients were coming along as expected. Dr. Clark, the veterinarian had X-rayed Gabe and found two more metal fragments. They were removed and his condition improved significantly. Maybe it was the regular cookie he had each day from "Doc Frost." Michael was informed that he would be ready to be transported by week's end. That news got Paul out of bed to shuffle in the hall a bit. In Aloha, Kenny had his landscape sub grade a six foot wide path around the perimeter of the property. On it he spread a layer of crushed gravel and on top of that a layer of cedar bark mulch. It would be a useful quarter mile walking path. He also planted a couple hundred white and purple Foxglove flowers and as many pink Lupine. The news carried a report of a fire that heavily damaged the Hillsboro Zion Evangelic Church. An investigation was looking into the possibility of arson as a hate crime.

On the third of May the UPS truck pulled into the covered garage and Michael helped offload the crate, which had a Purple

Heart medal fastened to it. He snapped a leash onto the big dog's collar understanding that it had been a tough day for him. A selected spot near the corner of the path was designed for Gabe to relieve himself. It and the doggy treat cookie were appreciated as a greeting to his new assignment. Gabe had a bit of trouble walking without toes on his left foot, but a bit of a limp was the only tell-tale sign of his injuries. Dr. Clark had advised Michael to walk Gabe on his right side. That way, Gabe's constant contact with his left shoulder on Michael's leg gave him ample vision on the right side. By the time they finished the quarter mile circuit Gabe was ready to be introduced to his new quarters, especially the soft cushion bed placed in his crate in the spare room. The removal of the gate, a bucket of water and a large bowl of kibbles was all the evidence he needed that this would be an acceptable posting. When Michael offered him a quarter of a Snicker Doodle Gabe wagged his tail in acceptance and settled down for a much needed nap. He still missed Doc Frost of course, but maybe in time that might be healed too.

The only ones not overjoyed with Gabe's arrival were Alice and Amanda. Apparently they had found a safe place to hide in either Cele or Cam's rooms, or maybe both. No one saw them all evening or the next morning.

Michael took Gabe for another walk by 0700. Happily, the black Shepherd knew what to do and where to do it. The training of this intelligent dog was evident. Michael smiled knowing that if this happened four times a day they would both have a mile of exercise. When they went back inside, Michael introduced him to the big cushion bed in the video room. It was pushed up against the west window wall and gave the promise of a sun blessed afternoon and a sweeping surveillance opportunity for one who was trained to be vigilant.

You know, the really odd thing was that about an hour later, Alice came out of hiding and slowly eased herself to the edge of the video room. She stayed there for at least an hour, studying this enormous monster that had invaded her home. Then very cautiously she approached Gabe. He probably watched her approach with his one eye, but he didn't move. She stood just out of his strike zone for a bit, then began purring and rubbed against his muzzle. Michael could hardly believe it and Noell began weeping. It was as if Alice had declared peace and Gabe had agreed. He didn't move at all. Alice moved a bit so she could cuddle near his warm neck and she rubbed him again and layed down. It truly was amazing. When the children came home from school, Cele was interested, Cam was cautious and Caleb was immediately endeared by a dog that had been in battle and was healing from his wounds. Gabriel had met the entire family and they had made him welcome.

Noell called Paul to tell him about the safe arrival of Gabe and the ideal situation he is enjoying. She was sure he understood that she was trying to encourage him to join them. What she wasn't able to tell him was about Gabe's enjoyment of all the music these children made. He was pleasantly calmed by it all.

At the conclusion of the 1100 dog-walk, Michael introduced Gabe to the food court thinking that there might be a broken Snicker Doodle or two. Actually he had noticed the Aloha PD cruiser parked out front and he was checking to make sure there was no problem. He found four tables occupied; one with two patrolmen.

"Good morning Cheryl. I want you to meet Gabriel. He's a service dog from Iraq." It was pleasant to be surrounded by positive folks who were interested in the newcomer.

"Kenny told me he was arriving," she said brightly. "He also said his nickname is 'Cookie Monster.'" The Shepherd's tail signaled recognition of a favorite word.

"Yeah, I'm afraid he is going to be your most loyal customer. I'd like to start a tab for the broken cookies. He's apparently not picky about the selection." They chuckled but Gabe continued to walk to the front window, and he lay down beside the police officers. Michael followed him over to the front table to introduce himself.

"Good morning gentlemen. I see Gabriel has found a uniformed group to join. He was a service dog attached to a Corpsman in Iraq.

You can see that he survived an IED. His handler is still in the Baltimore VA hospital. I'm Michael Winter." He shook their hands. "Officer Stanton," he had noticed the nametag on an officer who had responded to the con man's arrest, "I recognize you from a couple months ago."

"Yeah, I came to church the following Sunday. I was curious how this school and church work together." The warm smile suggested that it was a friendly curiosity.

"As a matter of fact," Michael wanted to give the brief explanation, "it is neither a church or a school. When the Aloha Christian had a fire just before Easter they needed an emergency place to meet for worship. They are here for four or five more Sundays and then their remodel will be finished. This is not a school either; it is the future home of the Aloha Youth Symphony. There are a dozen or so independent music teachers who meet with their students here during the week and a dance instructor is teaching two tap dance classes. Mr. Klein who is second chair violin in the Portland Symphony is organizing fifty or sixty kids to play together. We hoped to give a wholesome safe place for them to gather. It's just a place for kids." He thought of one more thing. "Cheryl, who runs the deli, is the wife of the contractor who built the place. She' here three or four hours a day, depending on the crowd. I'm glad to meet you both and hope this might be a regular lunch place for you."

He turned and patting the side of his leg, commanded: "Let's go Gabriel!" The Shepherd only looked at him. "Cookie Monster, with me! Doc Frost has a treat for you. Come on!" he commanded again. Slowly the large dog rose and obediently followed. Michael pondered how they could work on a better response.

Cheryl smiled as she handed a small paper sack to Michael. "There were only two broken Snicker Doodles, but I'll keep my eyes open for more tomorrow." Her cheerfulness was a happy part of the morning.

Noell had a huge smile as she talked with Paul. It was their mid-afternoon –Baltimore-time phone call. He had just informed her that he had been fitted with a light back brace that he could wear under his shirt and his knee brace was almost as convenient. The doctors had told him that they need his bed for another patient so he is free to make travel plans. He gratefully agreed that Portland was his number one choice to continue rehab and physical therapy. The Navy had given him a first class ticket for a late morning flight. Michael asked to talk with him before she hung up.

"Hi Doc. That's great news. We'll be happy to see your smiling face at the airport. Hey, Gabe and I are doing fine with my limited handling experience. Can you tell me the command for him to walk with me? We were in the food court and he flopped down by a couple police officers and I couldn't get him to budge until I bribed him with a cookie."

Paul chuckled at the idea of Michael's challenge. "I'll bet they had some GSR from the gun range or stepped in some residue accelerant in the shop. Shoes are a magnet for trace evidence. If he lies down it is a signal that he has located a possible problem. The command, 'Break' will tell him that he's free to continue the sweep." His voice broke into happy laughter, "But a cookie will do just as well with that sweet tooth." They chatted just a bit more before promising to see one another in two days.

When Caleb came home from School he did not go into the food court for a cookie with chocolate milk, he went to his dad's office for advice. "Dad, I need some more of your help," he began the conversation.

"How can I help you, Buddy?" Michael asked.

Caleb stepped into the office and closed the door. Obviously this was going to be a private conversation. Quietly he began, "I still have girlfriend problems."

For a moment Michael felt like a priest or a marriage counselor. "What sort of problems are you having, Pal?" He made sure there was no sign of the humor he was feeling, because one of them was very serious.

"I took your advice." Caleb began. "I listened and said nice things, you know, compliments, just like you said."

"And that didn't work?" the dad asked.

"Oh it worked too well," the agitated lad answered. "Today I got four notes from girls who think I'm going to be their boyfriend or something. They are acting like I am someone important. Carrey knows that I'm not but she always acts like I am. Sybil and Monica asked if they could have tickets for the program like I run the place, and Alison wants my help to join the orchestra. They act like I'm important." He shook his head in frustration.

"No Caleb. I think these young ladies are showing you that they know how important music is to you. It is something they would like to share. I remember something my dad used to say: 'It's nice to be important, but it's more important to be nice.' Friends share things, so why don't you and Carrey tell Sybil and Monica that the seats are free ones. They should come early for selection and ask Alison what instrument she plays. Maybe you could introduce her to Mr. Klein if she is serious. Those are the sort of things friends do."

"But dad, I don't want to break someone's heart. What if I do it wrong?"

Now Michael did chuckle. "You told me to remember that you are in the fourth grade. We are not talking romance here but honest friendship. Be nice. Get Carrey to help you include these young ladies in a way that will honor them and you. Who knows in ten years one of them might turn out to be romantic after all. If that happens ask your mom for advice. I'm still working on the serious stuff myself." Once again he ruffled Caleb's curly hair and gave him a hug.

In the coziness of their room, Noell was still concerned with all the details of Paul's arrival. She had gone over the list repeatedly. "Tomorrow can't get here soon enough," she said guardedly. "I'm just worried this isn't going to work out as smoothly as I hope," she finally said near tears.

"Sweetheart," Michael whispered as he put his arm around her, "we'll make it work. It's just a matter of making the right choices."

Against his chest her trembling voice asked, "But what if something happens that we aren't thinking about?"

"We always have choices," he whispered. 'Life lets us choose whether we are going to be a creator or a critic, a builder or a wrecker, a giver or a taker." He was quiet for a moment, then offered, "Let me rub your back a bit. That helps you relax."

"Mmmmm," she sighed. "That does feel good. A breath or two later she rolled over and said, "Mmmmm, that feels even better."

It was a warm spring morning with enough scattered clouds to allow plenty of scattered sunshine. The Foxglove were beginning to bloom in a riotous blanket and the Lupine were promising spikes. It would be their turn next. The 0700 walk had been invigorating. Gabe seemed to be adapting to his lack of toes. The 1100 walk was being accomplished with company. Noell volunteered to walk with him and they were surprised to have a few neighbors also using the path.

Michael said he was going to check on the broken cookies in the food court. He had noticed the Aloha Police cruiser parked out front. Noell thought she would take another lap. "Remember," she said happily, "Pauly's flight arrives at one o'clock.

"You're in luck this morning," Cheryl said as the duo entered. "There were two Snicker Doodles broken." Michael stopped at the cash register but Gabe strolled over to the front window and layed down by officer Stanton, who had a different partner.

Michael approached their table with a, "Good morning gentlemen. I hope you are enjoying Cheryl's deli."

The new officer said, "This is great, and there is no crowd. I'm Pat Gilman." He held out his hand.

Mr. Stanton made no effort to return Michael's greeting but snorted, "I see your dog hasn't learned much obedience. Maybe that explosion affected his brain." The words were bad enough but the tone of voice was snarky. He chuckled at his own humor.

Before Michael said something he might regret later, he said he hoped they enjoyed their lunch and commanded, "Gabriel, Break." The Shepherd rose immediately and accompanied Michael through the double doors.

He was still fuming about the officer's lack of civility a few minutes later. Noell suggested that since they only had a few more minutes before they went to meet Paul's flight, he might want to change the subject. Just then the double doors opened and the two police officers entered their home.

"We thought we'd take a peek at the rest of the building to see what else goes on back here," Stanton said. His tone was probably acceptable but since Michael was still a bit agitated, it wasn't acceptable.

"Stanton," Michael barked, "this is our residence. You've got no business in here." He didn't mean it to be cordial and the officers understood that immediately.

"Don't get on your high horse, Pal. There are no signs that say 'Private' so I was just curious."

"Yeah and remember what that got the cat." Michael had no intention to put up with his disrespect.

"Is that a threat Mr..." There would probably have been more but the other officer intervened.

"We're very sorry, Mr. Winter. We were out of line to open your door. We'll be on our way now. We're sorry for any inconvenience." He was guiding officer Stanton back out the door.

When they were out of earshot from each other, the police officer said to Stanton, "I didn't want your hot temper to get us kicked out of this deli too. Damn, that was the best turkey sandwich I can remember." At the same time Noell was saying, "I think you haven't been getting enough exercise. I think you just wanted to get rid of some steam with Mr. Stanton."

Paul came off the concourse in a wheelchair. His uniform caught the attention of several folks who thanked him for his service. Three or four offered to shake his hand and one gray haired man gave him a twenty dollar bill and said, "I'd like to buy you a beer later. Welcome home." He saluted and said 'Semper fi." Paul thanked him with a returning salute. At the baggage carousel folks stepped aside so his duffle bag could be retrieved and the port police officer blocked traffic to enable Michael to get to the curb for Paul's convenience. "Wow, I feel like a rock-star," the young man said with a smile. "This is a terrific home-coming for sure."

Noell smiled happily as she said, "We're glad it feels like a home-coming for you."

It took a bit less than three hours to get Paul comfortably settled in a guest suite. While Noell supervised the reunion with Gabriel, Michael said he had some business to attend to. She continued the conversation about Portland highlights then introduced him to his nieces and nephew. Michael called the only number he had for Randall. When that familiar voice answered, Michael had trouble convincing him that he was still retired. No he wasn't interested in a little spare cash now and then. Finally Randall said, "Who do you want me to look up for you? You must have some private action going on."

"Your right about that, bro," Michael said. "There is an Aloha cop that has triggered my bomb dog on two separate occasions. On top of that there have been three or four arson fires in churches of the area. This cop rubs me wrong. I just wonder if we have any file for a D. J. Stanton from Hillsboro Oregon. I haven't been able to get any listing for him from the directory and I don't want to make him suspicious. You've got my number if you run onto any intel."

To keep the conversation friendly, Michael asked, "Hey bro, are you any closer to getting that dance studio? I'm telling you, we've got some space if you want to get it started. There is already a lady here who is teaching tap dance lessons. I'd like to see your ugly mug. I miss you brother." Michael was sure that if Stanton was in the system, there would be ample information.

Friday evening was a pizza supper with an entire evening of chatting with Paul. He told them about his motivation for being a medic and his satisfaction in bringing healing to injured brothers. He had almost finished four tours in Iraq.

Saturday afternoon was the dress rehearsal for the Aloha Youth Symphony at 2:00 p.m. Cheryl demonstrated her resolve to place her deli before the community. She stayed open all afternoon until she ran out of food at 6:30.

The rehearsal was over and Michael was turning out the lights of the auditorium. He peeked around the curtain just to make sure all the folks had left when once again he saw her seated by the side aisle. Dressed in black she didn't move as he came down the steps. Once again he approached her slowly and asked if she was well.

"Oh my, yes, Papa. I am just so full of delight I want to listen a bit more to the echo. You have done a wondrous thing!" she said softly. "No one would imagine this great victory for music, and it is done with children!" He thought she was about to weep. Mrs. Gleason reached out her hand to him. "You are our hero, sir. That is also why I hesitate leaving this temple of joy." He carefully held her cold soft hand, "I must warn you that Till Eulenspiegel has returned. We thought that he had been defeated. It was his evil hand that set the blaze to our quarters. I'm sure of that. Poor Erma could not escape." A tear traced down her cheek until she dried it with a tissue. "But now I have concern for your safety, and the twins. They must be protected. Papa, you must be vigilant. I believe he is very close and has evil plans."

Michael was about to reassure her that many had tried unsuccessfully to overtake him. Instead, she said, "I can feel the strength of your heart. Soon you will have the opportunity to strike him. Do not hesitate nor try to give him consideration. He will be fighting to the death, as must you." She began to slowly stand. It was plain that she was in discomfort. "May we attend the inaugural presentation of the Youth Symphony next Monday? You know, that will be the fateful day."

Michael started to say, "You are always welcome here.' But Mrs. Gleason was already several steps up the aisle. Their conversation was again too brief and very difficult to comprehend. He decided to say nothing about this to Noell. But for sure he was going to be vigilant.

Sunday was Aloha Christian Church worship and then fellowship afterward. Michael took the family to dinner at the Chart House. Paul continued to be impressed with Portland, even though a large river flows through the center of it and seven bridges cross it. When Michael drove past the Riverside Center for Medical Education Paul was speechless. Michael told him, "The second floor is the Portland branch of the University of Oregon Med School. Dr. Titus Nichols is looking forward to your contact just as soon as the dust settles. I think you are going to be pleased with his suggestion."

"You folks are taking awfully good care of me," Paul said sincerely.

"Yeah, I'm trying to get your dog to like me," Michael chuckled.

Finally, Monday morning Randall returned Michael's request for information.

"Hey Mike, you called it on this character. The Army had a Dennis Justin Stanton who was section 8 out of the service in '94." He gave Michael a Hillsboro address. "He was involved in two arson fire investigations that could never be proven. A warehouse and an Elks Club burned under suspicious circumstances. When he set fire to a Camp Pendleton hillside there were witnesses. The fire was contained before it got out of control but it was enough for him to be sectioned out. There seems to be a lengthy list of part time watchman, security sort of jobs. I can't figure out how he got past a background check from a reliable police hire, unless he buried his Army records under a couple dozen rent-a-cops. There is no record of arrests or warrants. He's just a very unstable person. Be careful, man. You know the sections can go off for the littlest reason.

"Now about that dance studio; I'm going to be in Seattle next month. Do you have a vacancy I can hang with for a couple days? I want to see Noell again. Man, she was some kind of cute. I'll give you a shout in a couple weeks for the details."

When Mr. Klein came to Harmony House Monday afternoon he told Michael about finding an Aloha police officer in the back of the stage. "Apparently he was just inspecting the place, but he gave me the Willies," the director said.

Lunch time on Tuesday was an opportunity for Michael to watch for the Aloha cruiser. When he made sure that Mr. Stanton was going to the food court, he quickly drove to Hillsboro and found the isolated address Randall had given him. A knock on the door brought no response, even from a dog so Michael peered in the available windows and tried the door to the detached garage. Everything seemed secure even if it was pretty dated. He went to the garbage can and examined some discarded junk-mail addressed to Dennis Stanton. Then he hurried back to Harmony House.

The excitement for the weekend grew more demanding each day. Caleb practiced the introduction so often his mom finally asked him to rehearse in the auditorium. Cam had been named first chair violin and Cele was right beside her. At last the final bit of preparation was attended to. Mr. Klein distributed black T shirts to every musician. The black shirts had a silk-screened white necktie and an *AYS* Aloha Youth Symphony, making them look formal and uniform. The director sternly said, "Do not wear this shirt before the concert. I want them clean and fresh. After the concert they are yours to treasure as the beginning of a legend." Just in time, Memorial day dawned clear and promising. There was time to go through the musical selections once more.

Cheryl took advantage of the expected crowd by offering a deli lunch special and an extended after-program Italian supper of Lasagna or Minestrone soup with bread sticks.

Michael was just finishing Gabe's 3 p.m. walk. They had hurried a bit so Michael could join Noell and Paul in the front row. This was an exciting culmination of two year's labor. As the elevator door opened in the covered garage, Gabe hesitated, then he began backing away. Michael encouraged him to get in the elevator, but the Shepherd was not about to cooperate. Instead he tugged back and edged toward the furnace room door. Michael's frustration was ready to use the "Break" command. They vanished, however, when he noticed the pry marks on the door, and Gabriel layed down and waited.

Carefully Michael opened the door, his training now on full alert. There were no wires or triggers, but at the side of the large furnace was box that was clearly out of place. Someone had placed it strategically under the gas line. Carefully Michael examined it also for wires or triggers, then gently lifted the lid. It was definitely a bomb, albeit a primitive one, a large one with a timer counting down the seconds. It was set to explode in one hour and twenty two minutes, just when the symphony would be in progress directly above the furnace room. In a moment of understanding, Michael knew who had placed the devise and what should be done with it. He backed out of the room, told Gabe to "Break" and took him upstairs.

Acting as normal as possible, Michael told Noell he had one quick errand to run. "Save me a seat," was all he said as he kissed her and hurried out. The heavy box was placed in the back of the Range Rover and within fifteen minutes was repositioned against the back wall of Mr. Stanton's home, with eight hours added to the timer. He was back in the auditorium as Mr. Klein, the conductor, was being applauded.

Cam played a long tuning note and as the rest of the orchestra tuned, she and Cele played an additional nine note chord. The room became silent as the conductor raised his baton. The Aloha Youth Symphony began playing Edvard Grieg's *Morning* from *Peer Gynt* Incidental Music Op. 23. They were young, inexperienced and wonderful. The room was charmed. After a brief pause, Mr. Klein introduced Camille Saint-Saens' *The Swan* from the Carnival of the Animals. After a brief intermission the children returned to play Edward Elgar's *Nimrod*, which means hunter. They concluded with "*God Bless America*" to a standing ovation. There was no encore except a nine note cord played by the first and second violins. A frequently asked question by the folks who were leaving the auditorium was, "How can we get a copy of the KOIN tape?" Michael thought a disc copy would be a great promotional idea.

When the room was nearly empty Michael went to the side aisle to once again greet Mrs. Gleason and the two other ladies with her. "I believe we were all delighted that those children could fill this hall with such beauty," he said softly.

Mrs. Gleason answered just as softly, "If you don't mind we would relish a bit of reflection before we leave. They were so charming." The other two nodded in agreement.

Michael leaned in close to Mrs. Gleason so he could whisper, "I believe Till has been thwarted. We'll see what the night brings." She had nothing more to say, but patted his strong shoulder.

The food court was filled for the second time after the concert. Rusty James waved Michael and family over to a vacant table beside them. Carrey was still very excited by their success. She even gave hugs to Cele, Cam and especially Caleb. "Wasn't that just wonderful?" she bubbled. They all had observations to make about the performance. The chatting stopped when Kenny brought out a tray with six generous portions of Lasagna and bread sticks.

The morning news reported an East Hillsboro house fire. The home, was owned by an Aloha police officer who was under investigation for fireworks violations. First information was scarce because two secondary explosions had made it impossible for the firemen to get near enough the structure to effectively fight the blaze. Ultimately the house was reduced to ashes. They had protected the nearest home and the detached garage. Subsequent investigation had found bomb making material in the garage and evidence from four previous church fires and suspicion that Central Lutheran of Beaverton and Cornerstone Presbyterian Church of Hillsboro were also targeted. The identity of the lone victim will be made from dental records.

"Good morning Mr. Frost. I'm glad to meet you at last. I see your injuries are healing." Dr. Nichols chuckled, "I feel like we have already met. Your brother-in-law is a persistent man with surprising connections. I'm not sure how he found out that during your tour of duty you had occasion to work with six of our graduates. All six of them have sent me a letter of recommendation on your behalf. If you can confirm even half of their testaments we'll be well on our way here." The two men shook hands.

"Thank you for seeing me, sir. I know the summer session is ready to begin. I'm just hoping we can map out a plan for a future place for me." Paul slid a journal across the desk . "This is a journal of the procedures I did in Iraq. I don't suppose scorpion stings happen very often here, nor eye flushes from blown sand." They both enjoyed his relaxed humor.

"Can you tell me what your eventual goals might be," the president asked.

A wide smile answered, "I am convinced my life will be spend in some form of physical assistance. I have imagined myself as an EMT, a trauma nurse or a therapist. The highest goal is to be a trauma nurse or doctor, Paul said. His eyes held Dr. Nichol's confidently.

The president placed his hand on the journal saying, "There are far too many bullet wounds in here. All six of your Field Surgeons report that you are too talented to be a trauma nurse. In several emergency situations they only had to approve the job you had done for them. That is remarkable. Give me a couple days to go through this and we can talk again." He glanced at his calendar. "How about Thursday morning? I have a light schedule; can you be here by nine?" Just that easy his academic program was underway.

While that conference was taking place, Michael was having another one at Harmony House. A black limo parked in the front and an attorney rang the double door bell. For just a moment Michael wondered if he had left any trace at the Hillsboro house. He took a deep breath to calm his nerves and opened the door. The attractive woman was dressed in black and wore a brilliant smile. She introduced herself saying "I'm Lisle Chambers, legal counsel for Elva Gleason. May I have a bit of your time to set an important, meeting with her?"

As Michael listened he was thinking, "with a smile like that I'll bet she wows a lot of jurors." But he said, "Can you tell me the nature of the meeting? Mrs. Gleason has been supportive of the children's music activities here, but I can't imagine what might require legal counsel.

There was that smile again. Michael thought that Ms. Chambers knew full-well the power it had so his guard was increased. She answered lightly, "It is no sinister matter, I assure you, sir. As you must have noticed last Monday, Elva, her younger sister Ida, and cousin Ada are getting along in age. They would like to make a proposal that may be mutually beneficial. She is hoping that you might allow me to drive you to their Cherry Gove home. It is only a few minutes west."

"Are you suggesting that we go today?" he asked for clarity.

"Why yes," she answered brightly, "now would be a perfectly marvelous time." He grimaced a bit, aware that she had out maneuvered him nicely.

Michael wrote a quick note to Noell explaining where he was going and the plan to return before Cheryl closed the deli. The limo driver went eight miles west and then seven miles southwest. All the while Ms. Chambers kept a steady stream of questions to Michael. She asked about his service time, which didn't take long to explain. She asked how he had met Noell and why had they moved to Portland. There was the plausible answer, which he used instead of the truth. She had several questions about Harmony House. Just before they arrived at Cherry Grove, it became apparent that she wanted to control the conversation and kept herself out of it.

The driver pulled into a tree-lined lane and stopped in front of a house with a winding walk, and the charred scar of a recent fire on the back corner. A noisy confrontation was in progress. A man with a shotgun was standing on the porch while three angry men were urging him to get out of the way. As soon as the limo stopped the three moved a short ways away sullenly.

Michael immediately got out of the car and walked toward the men asking, "Is there a problem here?"

"If there is," one of them snarled, "it's none of your business."

"It wouldn't take much more than that wise-crack to make it my business." Michael continued to move toward them squared up for a quick strike.

The largest of the three recognized the posture of attack and urged the other two to get back into their car. "We'll be back tough guy. Then we'll make it your business." The three hurried into their car and quickly left.

Ms. Chambers looked into his eyes and said "Thank you. I see why Elva believes in you so fervently." She beckoned him into the house where the shotgun carrier had disappeared.

Mrs. Gleason greeted him by saying, "Papa, now you see. Till Eulenspiegel is knocking at my door. He has vicious intent. Thank you for coming to my protection."

Michael looked at Ms. Chambers who was no longer smiling. She simply shrugged.

He said, "I was confused. When I told you that Till had been thwarted, I was speaking about a separate problem. Tell me what these men want."

Mrs. Gleason asked him to be seated and poured him a cup of tea. "It is a lengthy story, Papa," the soft voice began. "In 1921 when I was a small girl, my family moved here with six other families to make a collective farm. My father, the policeman, was a competent grape grower. He planted fifty acres. Two other families planted fifty acres of cherry trees and two more had fifty acres of table vegetables. One family set up large chicken houses and the other raised beef and hogs. There were casual neighbors who took advantage of this flat fertile soil with smaller farms. We enjoyed one another's assistance with harvests and frequently bartered for meat or milk. As that pioneer generation aged we looked after each other and as they died off those who had no children to pass the inheritance along, did the next best thing. The collective became more condensed. Ida, Ada and I are the last survivors of the 200 acres. A large commercial farm has been trying to convince us to leave. He has offered to buy us at about a quarter of the value of the land. Now he is using intimidation."

"Recently the pressure has turned violent, as you just saw. Two of our employees have been hospitalized and four more have just been frightened away. Daniel is our last defense. He is the grandson of my father's foreman."

Ms. Chambers took over by saying, "We have a plan that is desperate. It involves you in a surprising way. Mrs. Gleason has suggested that we Quit Claim the property to you, sir. That way they have nothing to sell and the realtor's aggressive efforts will be more public. She has suggested that the property be held in a trust until your children are adults; then the property and the violins will still be together. Their only request is that you allow them to continue to live on this property as long as possible. Do you have any questions or comments?"

"I have a considerable number of both," Michael said. "But my most immediate question is about these harassing visits. Did you say they happen at night?"

Elva nodded slowly, "Almost every night, sometimes twice if they are especially wound up. They frequently throw things at the house, two windows have been broken." Her shoulders slumped in dejection.

Michael said "We can talk about the property later. First I need to put a stop to the harassment. Daniel," he called to the man who was standing behind the door to the kitchen.

The curly haired man no longer carried his shotgun. He stepped out of the shadows hesitantly.

"Daniel," Michael said cordially, "what can you tell me about their farm? Does the manager live there? Are there houses or cabins for the help?"

"I've only been by it once," the soft voice answered, but I think the south end of the large building is the main office and maybe the manager lives there. There are four or five tough men who stay upstairs. The rest of that building is their power equipment.

"Are there other homes or farms nearby?" Michael was trying to formulate a battle plan.

Daniel shook his head and replied "None signore."

"One more question," Michael said with a smile. "How far is the big building from here?"

"Maybe two miles, straight down this road," he gestured and replied.

Michael said in a calm voice, "We can talk about the property at a more convenient time. Ms. Chambers if you will be kind enough to drive me home. I need to get some tools. I'm assuming that the hornets have been aroused enough to be angry when they come back. They may have a surprise. I'll join you ladies for supper, if I may."

It was after nine o'clock and the lights were all turned off inside the house. Michael had told them to rest assured that he would keep them safe as he patrolled the shadows outside. The pick-up didn't even try to be quiet as it thundered to a stop. Two jumped out of the bed shouting, "Get those witches!" and two more stepped out of the cab. It appeared that the only weapons were a couple of baseball bats. Michael had carefully kept a large landscape shrub between him and them, for concealment. When the truck lights went off he went into action.

The two that jumped out of the back of the truck went straight toward the house up the winding sidewalk. Before they got there four silenced .22 rounds had found the back of the heads of the driver and passenger. Michael quickly positioned the bodies back in the truck. They sort of looked normal. He put in a fresh clip and waited for the other two to react. As they ran back toward the truck they each caught two rounds in the chest. He put their bodies in the bed of the pickup and drove it away.

It wasn't hard to find the big building. It looked like every light was on inside and outside. This was an unknown battlefield. Michael stopped before he got near the building to quickly weigh his options. He noticed the large elevated gas tank and made his plan. With a shirt ripped off one of the casualties he made a long wick that went down the fuel pipe. He wedged a lifeless leg against the throttle, lit the wick and pulled the pickup into gear. He rolled out of the way as it gained momentum. It first hit the legs on the end of the elevated gas tank and then slammed into the big building. A bloom of orange flame erupted as the tank fuel found ignition from the wick and then another explosion as the pickup's tank let go. It was obvious that this place was going to get real hot real quick. Michael headed for the dark shadows away from the holocaust and stayed well off the road. It took over ten minutes for the first emergency vehicle to streak down the road. He was almost back to Elva's home. After another three minutes a fire truck appeared and Michael was standing beside his own car. By then the big building and all the expensive farm equipment in it was fully engaged; the entire building would be a total loss.

As he drove home Michael pondered those past minutes. It was a familiar battlefield emotion. He pondered about the sudden end of four lives. He was neither happy or sad for them. They had entered into a conflict ignorantly. He felt remorse because he was sure that Noell would be completely against his actions. She had felt that way even when it was her life and her children's that he had rescued. He wondered how Elva might feel about this sudden change. By the time he got home he had fairly succeeded in pushing those thoughts out of his mind, but he knew they would come back.

In the welcome darkness of their room, she felt him come to bed, but neither of them whispered, "good night." They lay in strained quiet unaware that the other was also wrestling with feelings of longing. Finally she willed herself to go to sleep. An hour later, maybe more, she heard distinctly a woman's voice speak in the darkness, "Noell." Then after a long silence, she heard it again, "Noell." She strained to hear more but the room was as it should be, peacefully still. She looked at the clock on the night stand; it was half past one.

"You were late last night." Noell's soft voice was not asking a morning question.

"Mrs. Gleason is having some trouble with an aggressive real-estate developer," he answered. "She asked if I could be a bit of security for them." He was hesitant to say more.

"Did they get a dose of what Uncle Phillip received?" she asked softly.

"Something like that. I had to be sure it wouldn't happen again."

Tears filled Noell's eyes as she whispered, "I'm sorry for them, and you. I'll wager they didn't even see it coming." The tears spilled down her cheeks. "I know it was self defense. You were only protecting the vulnerable ones. But I think about those young men who never had a chance to know the tenderness of a child's kiss, never realized some achievement, never had a chance to grow old with another." A sob shook her small frame.

Michael was quiet for a long while and then said, "They chose a very dangerous path."

"Yes, I know it was self-defense sort of," Noell whispered with a shudder. "On one hand they deserve what they got. On the other hand, you know that you crossed the line again.

Michael was silent, knowing that she was speaking the truth. He felt the pain of the one he loved. Changing the subject he told her,

"Mrs. Gleason was so distraught over the harassment that she has been getting that she is thinking about turning her 200 acre farm over to a trust fund for our children, just to get that buyer off her back." He thought a big subject might deflect the more painful other one that neither of them wanted to visit. "She had her attorney there to talk to me about a Quit Claim and a deed of Trust for the kiddos."

"What?" Noell said in an incredulous voice. She dried her eyes and asked, "Why in the world would she do such a thing?" She was still for a moment then asked, "Is she that desperate or is it because of the violins?"

He breathed a sigh of relief before replying, "I'm sure she must feel desperate. Growing old with few resources must cause panic. She did mention that she hoped to keep them together." It was enough to end that conversation. But they both harbored echoes of those words. They were both convinced that today they were less in tune with the other. Something major had come between them.

Then Ms. Chambers called. Michael had barely said "hello" when she asked "Jesus, Michael! Are you some kind of Ninja? Five dead! Apparently the manager was caught up in the fire too. That blaze destroyed a couple million dollars worth of building and an equal amount in the equipment. The Fire Marshal has determined that the driver of the pickup lost control and clipped the fuel tank before plowing into the garage. Under the collapsed rubble there is hardly enough of them left to identify. Brother! Did you ever take care of the problem?!"

She continued, "Mrs. Gleason wants to finish our conversation as soon as possible. She has advised me that time is critical if we want to get all the signatures. Apparently her younger sister Ida has a medical situation. When can we meet in my office?" She paused as though weighing some important options. "Perhaps a better alternative would be to meet in your food court. I understand the deli turkey sandwiches are the best in the city."

Michael was not real excited about meeting with the attorney again at all. Defensively he said, "The lady who prepares those sandwiches is only here from 11 o'clock to about three."

"Oh that is such a good suggestion," Ms. Chambers giggled. "We'll be there by eleven so save us a good table."

"Damn!" Michael thought. "She did it to me again."

Noell loved it when he kissed her goodnight and then held her until she felt his breathing become deep and slower. Sometimes there was even a relaxing twitch. She closed her eyes and gave thanks for perfect tranquility. She couldn't imagine her life being any better as she gently drifted into sleep.

"Noell." In the darkness the voice sounded again near and soft. Michael was still sleeping soundly. "Noell, you are chosen," the voice whispered. She waited for several minutes to hear more, but only silence danced in the darkness. She looked at the clock; once again it was half past one.

At eleven o'clock Michael was sitting in the food court watching Paul walk Gabe around the perimeter. He saw the limo turn in the driveway and told Noell, who was chatting with Cheryl, that the crowd was arriving. Just moments later the elevator doors opened and a sweet lady with an enormous smile came in.

"Papa, our champion!" Elva cried out. "Our precious champion!" She was with the other three ladies who made their way to the table set for six.

Elva first held Michael's hand, then embraced him as she would a family member. "Thank you, sir. Till is no longer knocking at our door." She was practically giggling.

Embarrassed by her accolade, Michael introduced Noell. "Sweetheart, let me introduce Elva's sister Ida and her cousin Ada." Noell shook their fragile hands. "And this prominent looking attorney is Lisle Chambers." With another handshake they all sat down.

Cheryl came over to take their beverage orders. She told them that the Peach Iced Tea was paired with the turkey sandwiches, so they all agreed to try it.

Once seated, Elva looked directly at Noell and said, "Please do not feel harsh about what he has done to protect us. It makes me tremble to think of the terrible deeds planned for us. Michael, like a sheltering angel stepped into our defense. I don't want to know how he did it. This is one of those times when ignorance is bliss. But this morning for the first time in months, we can relax and know that we are safe."

Her gentle words triggered the memories Noell carried. "Yes, I know that feeling too, she said in a whisper "The rational part of me wants to condemn the violence, but the blessed safety of my children and me feels the gratitude more." She squeezed his arm.

Cheryl brought out a tray with sandwiches and glasses of tea, as two more tables were seated. "It looks like this is going to be a busy lunchtime. Thanks for coming in early."

When the sandwiches were consumed and the glasses refilled, Lisle admitted with a sigh, "These sandwiches have my vote for best in the city for sure. I feel like these should accompany some special holiday. It pains me to admit that I am already planning when I can have lunch here again."

With a grin, Michael said, "Since there is no further danger at Cherry Gove, I'm wondering if this meeting is now necessary."

Elva looked at Lisle and replied, "I told you he would come to that conclusion." Then looking at Michael she went on, "The only thing that has changed is the urgency of yesterday. We still feel strongly that the ownership of the farm should no longer be our burden. We love it there, but are less and less able to properly care for it. We want to proceed with the Quit Claim if you are willing."

"Elva," Michael asked, "I noticed the fire damage to your house. Is that recent?"

Her face revisited the pains of a terrible night. The gentle woman said, "That was Erma's room. Four years ago a fire bomb was thrown through the window. She was trapped. We replaced the window but sealed off the room in sorrow. We haven't funds to repair it."

"Perhaps that is something that should be brought to the attention of the new owner, Michael said with a chuckle. "The contractor who made this wonderful place for us has many employees who will repair that room and any other needs your house might have." Michael had no memory of a grandmother, but the tender feelings he had for these women was near enough.

Ms. Chambers said quietly, "You know there are five other farm houses that are on the property. Daniel is living in one but the rest have been vacant for quite some time."

Without much hesitation, Michael said, "Then I guess Kenny Fox will have some extra work to do this summer. May we make an appointment to do an inspection?"

Ms. Chambers asked in her professional voice, "Is that a stipulation before you agree to the transfer of ownership?"

"Lord no," Michael snorted. "I just want to make sure these ladies have a safe comfortable home. I would do this in either case."

Ida spoke for the first time. Her voice was soft and warm. "We have for a long time believed that we are the last of the Oski (pronounced ooskee)." Looking at Noell she went on, "It may be that you are also one, or your twins perhaps. My heart rejoices in this discovery."

Noell shook her head in confusion. "I have no idea what that means."

"Till Eulenspiegel called us 'witches,' Ida answered. "Others have used the term 'Hags' But an Oski is a wish fulfiller and an Oskimey is a wish maiden. We help folks realize their dreams. Now you are doing that for us." She shyly looked down at the tablecloth.

Ada added, "When the farm was in its good years we had more than enough resources to share. These days we spend much time in prayer. It is our only available resource." Looking intently at Michael, she concluded, "For the last two years you have given us much to praise and raise prayers of gratitude. Now it would appear we have a fresh reason to give thanks." Her warm smile added to his sense of family.

Ms. Chambers brought them back to the task at hand. "I have a 2 o'clock appointment, so may I have you and Mrs. Winter sign these documents? The ladies have already signed and I have notarized them. I can still get them to the Escrow company today if you will provide a $2,600 check for the Title Insurance and transfer." When that simple detail was accomplished, she stood as a signal to the table that it was time to go.

Even though all the other tables were full, Elva patted her hand saying, "Just one more minute, please." When Lisle was again seated, she looked at Michael and said, "You once asked me about the history of the violins. I can only tell you that Erma and I received them in 1922 from Lawrence Schultz, whose sisters, Daphne and Dorothy had received them in '86. Lawrence was an evangelist who travelled to many churches in the area. I believe they lived on this very property until he was burned out by hooligans. Did you happen to find his history box?"

"Was it covered in a pile of rocks?" Michael asked, as he began to put things together.

"I don't know where it was hidden, I only know that it had a blessed Tau protecting it." She looked at him for several moments. When he didn't answer, she asked, "Why do you suppose you were attracted to this construction shamble? Many, many, people have passed this property and saw nothing but neglect. Yet in one day's time you saw the potential of Harmony House. I believe the Tau spoke to your heart; saw in you a champion who would care more for the children and us than profit." She looked more seriously into his brown eyes and asked, "Haven't you wondered how an old wooden box, that should have rotted and disintegrated long ago, could still be in pristine condition a century after it was buried? The Tau was blessed by the priestesses just as the violins were. Keep it close to your family and remarkable longevity will be yours and insight that will baffle you."

Shifting her gaze to the attractive face, she said, "Darling Noell, you may become the new seer. Your heart is pure and tender. You will be a confident follower."

Again looking at him she said, "You are our champion, Michal, and now our leader." She stood with considerable difficulty, kissed his hand and quietly said, "Papa". One by one they all stood, including Ms. Chambers; they kissed his hand devoutly and softly said, "Papa".

For much of the afternoon he replayed those conversations in his mind. He had no idea what Elva had in mind, but he was certain that Noell's words burned his conscience. "On one hand they deserve what they got. On the other hand, you know that you crossed the line again." It echoed in his mind. "you crossed the line *again*," Those words nagged at him. In spite of the fact that they were righteous hits, they caused her grief, which became grievous to him. In the Corps at times like this there was always an available chaplain to talk with; Michael called Pastor Carlson.

The pastor's office was comfortable and decorated with several pictures and articles of faith. If these feelings weren't so strong Michael would welcome some small talk about the meaning of some of them. Wisely the pastor didn't waste time with trivia.

"Michael, you said you were having some PTSD issues. Are these connected to your activity in the military?" The pastor's gaze was steady and serious.

"They started there but didn't end with my discharge. My extensive training was in what's called, 'black ops,' which means lethal action with little or no evidence. For thirteen years I was very skilled at it. In fact, I met Noell when those skills were needed to protect her and the kids. I had no more remorse than a pilot dropping a bomb on a target. It was just a job that needed doing."

The pastor said quietly, "That activity started in the Corps, but you've been out three years and it sounds like the activity has continued. Are there any wants or warrants for your arrest or are you a suspect for a crime?" His eyes searched Michael's.

With a look that was just as steady, Michael replied, "No sir, as I said, black ops is efficient and undetected. I will tell you that the person who set fire to your church had plans to detonate a bomb at Harmony House while the youth symphony was in performance. He died in a fire in his own home instead. Authorities determined that the fire was accidental, even though it was started with the bomb meant for us. He was a person with mental issues who never had a chance to find help. Therein lies the core of my guilt. Noell is a loving tender person who believes in compassion and assistance. I'm not."

The pastor was still for a moment, pondering his response. "It is about as difficult to absolve yourself of your own guilt as it is to sit on your own lap. In order to break the cycle of secrecy we need somebody before whom we can put away the disguise, trusting that when we are seen for what we truly are we will not be further condemned or rejected. With all my heart I believe that is the Lord's response to us, regardless of our guilt. He loves us absolutely, welcomes us absolutely and forgives us absolutely. The trust we find in that cleansing act is the seed of our faith in him. We learn to trust him for we no longer have a reason to feel guilty. Jesus said to the paralytic, 'Your sins are forgiven.' Then he said 'Rise and walk.' Where upon the man picked up his bed and went home. Whatever was holding him down was gone and he was free to walk a straight line.

"Michael, as much as we all would like to change the past, that is beyond our ability. But we can change our future by walking a new straight way. I sincerely believe that God has already forgiven you. That's the whole meaning of the cross. Now it is up to you to live like a forgiven person.

"But pastor," Michael struggled with the concept, "I haven't done anything to merit forgiveness. I just don't see how this works."

Pastor Carlson smiled warmly and said, "In the language of the print shop, 'Justify' means to set the type in such a way that all full lines are of equal length and flush on both right and left margins. In other words, the printed lines are in right relationship with the page and the other lines. In the religious sense when we are forgiven we are in right relation with God and one another. Paul says in Romans 5 that being justified means being at peace with God. He uses the noun 'Justification' for the first step in the process of holiness or wholeness."

Michael shook his head. "I still don't see what I have done to deserve that," he said in wonder.

"Well, buddy." The pastor said with a big smile. "It's not about your nature, but the nature of God. It is something only God can do. Paul," he looked at his listener to get a nod of recognition. "Paul was on his way to Damascus to round up Christians and destroy their fellowship when suddenly he heard the voice of the Risen Lord. Until that very moment he had been an adversary, a genuine pain and what you would expect the voice to say is, 'You are in such trouble.' But in effect what the voice did say was, 'I want you on my team'. Paul never got over it.

"As far as Paul was concerned, he was the last man in the world to deserve such an invitation like that. God, however, was revealing that it was precisely that sort of person he wanted, not because of who Paul was, but who God was. All the voice seemed to want Paul to do was believe that it meant what it said and do as it asked. Paul did both.

"At a moment in his life when he had least reason to expect it, Paul was staggered by the idea that no matter who you are or what you have done, God wants you on his side. There is nothing you have to do or be. It's on the house. God has justified you – lined you up. To feel this in your bones is the first step on the way to being forgiven. There is only one catch. Like any other gift, the gift of grace can be yours only if you reach out and take it."

Once again Michael shook his head in wonder. "To be so important, that just seems so very one sided. I have a mountain of hateful things to just have them wiped away it's too easy."

"Remember," the pastor said softly "it was not easy. The cross was a terrible challenge. But that love was given to make us right with God and others, to forgive your sins, those that were committed and those that were caused by omission, the loving opportunities you didn't take, the family members or moments of charity you have ignored. They are all cleansed as though they never happened."

For just a moment Michael thought of his brother and wondered what the clinic custodian was doing at this very minute. Just as quickly he pondered on his own future and his family's. "You've given me a lot to ponder. My conscience may be relieved but I'm not sure how that is going to affect my behavior." His gaze was fixed on the pastor's.

"Well Michael," he said lightly, "if you are looking for something like the twelve step road to holiness, we don't have that. Martin Luther said about four hundred years ago, 'Love God and do whatever you please.' I think that means if you love God, you will do just what pleases him. If God is Love, which we firmly believe, you will be most blessed when you are doing deeds of love and compassion. Does that make sense to you?"

"It is a clear beginning point, that's for sure. I think you will see a lot more of us as we figure out where we go from here. Thank you for your time." He stood and offered to shake the pastor's hand. "What's your hourly rate?" he asked with a smile."

"We'll figure that out after we see where we are going." Then the pastor asked, "Are you sure he set fire to our church?" with a voice that was increasingly dear to Michael.

"Yours and at least three others," he answered with a confident nod.

He found Noell in the kitchen preparing supper. She listened intently to his account with the pastor. She was fascinated by the content of their talk. It was the conclusion Michael had found that amazed her; he vowed to use his military skills only as last option in the protection of his family. The embrace she gave him was verification of starting on the right path. Then he told her that he was going to go out to that old pile of rocks and retrieve the wooden cross.

In the furnace room work bench he remembered the furniture polish and steel wool that they had used on the auditorium seats. In a few delightful moments the old wood took on a deep luster. The challenge would be in choosing a place to display it. Noell was quick to solve that question by saying she would like it hung on the wall opposing the bed in their room. "I can't think of a more positive help than to have my last thought at night and first in the morning of the symbol of His love for us." Michael drilled a small hole in the back and set a Molly bolt in the wall to display the Tau.

In an evening conversation with the family, Michael shared the story of the cross that protected the box that had hidden the story of the violins. The listeners all had questions that he couldn't answer, but hoped Mrs. Gleason might. The lingering fact was that each member made it a practice to visit the cross, to touch it on the way to bed and first thing every morning. Their simple pilgrimage had unique importance to each. The girls began placing their violin cases on the dresser at the foot of the cross. They had no way of knowing how, but they were convinced it helped them to play more beautifully.

June was a very busy month. It began with a conversation with Kenny Fox. Michael proposed an evaluation of the six Cherry Grove houses beginning with Elva's. "If they are restorable, let's see if we can make some high end remodeling."

Randall visited for two days, then returned two weeks later saying that the life Michael had found was just what Randall had dreamed of. He asked how he could find a place somewhere nearby.

Ed and Helen could not wait until Christmas to see Paul, and Noell, and Caleb an Camilla and Celia, and of course Michael. They were even eager to meet Gabriel who had saved their son's life. They had said they were staying for only a long weekend but the return flight home was for the following Tuesday, a week later.

Paul took all the med tests for the nursing program and aced them . He completed the test for second year med student and aced that. Doctor Nichols suggested he begin some specialty subjects, to which Paul answered immediately that orthopedics was his primary interest. He was told that as soon as he had the approval from the VA physical therapist he could begin his internship at Legacy.

Caleb had a Sunday recital to a nearly packed auditorium, and Cele and Cam invited a group of drummers from a Portland Irish tavern to join them for a night of Celtic fiddles. Cele demonstrated her new talent of clog stepping as she played and Caleb joined them as they played Yanni's *Until the Last Moment.* There was enough demand to hear it again that a second performance was scheduled the following Sunday.

Yes, it was a very busy month. As soon as school was out Mr. Klein increased the rehearsals of the youth symphony to two a week And through it all Michael and Noell were delighted that their music immersion plan had worked so well, so amazingly well. Through it all the three ladies from Cherry Grove were in faithful attendance.

"Noell." The voice was soft again but very clear. "Noell, come to us. Please join us." She looked at Michael's sleeping face. Serenely, he had not heard the voice. It was calling her alone. She looked at the clock; it was half past one, again. For just a moment she thought about ignoring it as ridiculous but she felt an urgency. Quietly she slipped out of bed and pulled on her blue running top and pants. She ruffled her hair as she found her keys then made her way to the garage and into the night. She was pretty sure whose voice she heard and how she could find the proper turns. About twenty minutes later she turned into the tree lined lane, right behind a black limo. Apparently Lisle had heard the voice as well. She stopped in front of the darkened house with the winding sidewalk.

Lisle entered the open door and a moment later Noell followed her into a room whose only light was five candles. Three women were standing around the small round table that held the candle holders.

Elva motioned Lisle to stand near them and then guided Noell to the last place.

"Thank you for following your heart to us," she spoke quietly to Noell. "This must seem quite strange to you. I still marvel when the circle is gathered. We have not been able since Erma's sad death, for there must always be five to make the star. This is the test."

She held her hands in front of her at arms' length saying, I am Courage." The candle in front of her flickered and then brightened significantly.

Ida standing next to her lifted her hands and said in a feather-soft voice, "I am Fidelity." Her candle also flickered and then brightened.

Ada, who stood on the other side of Elva said, "I am Wisdom." Once again there was a moment of hesitation and then her candle brightened.

Standing next to her, Lisle lifted her hands and said sweetly, "I am Mercy." Her candled brightened. Noell's heart was beating rapidly as she waited for instructions.

Elva had a broad smile as she looked at her and said as though in prayer, "Say you are Compassion."

Noell hesitated just a fluttering heartbeat. Then she raised her hands and said, "I am Compassion." Her candle flickered and then all five of the candles became bright enough to light the corners of the room distinctly.

"Sisters," Elva's voice nearly sang, "now we are five. Hold the hands of those beside you and gaze at the ceiling. Our shadows have made the star of the Oski. We are complete again." They all arched their backs to see the clear sign of a star on the ceiling. As they stood upright, Elva said in a blessing voice, "Sisters, follow your hearts."

Lisle released Noell's hand and kissed her on the cheeks saying, "My sister." She turned and exited silently. One by one the others followed, with kisses and the claim, "My sister." Finally Elva embraced her, delivered kisses and in a trembling voice said, "My sister." The five candles fluttered dark with tiny wisps of smoke. Noell turned toward the door and her drive home.

Gabe was waiting as the Harmony House elevator door opened. As soon as he identified her as one of his own, he turned back to his warm bed and she went to hers. Michael's deep regular breathing was a comfort to her, but the memory of those Cherry Gove minutes kept her awake for much of the rest of the night. "What had she become?"

Kenny was in the middle of a report on the Cherry Grove houses. "The one with the barn is salvageable, but just. The barn is in better condition. Mrs. Gleason was pretty adamant that she didn't want any changes to her house except maybe a new kitchen stove and one of those walk-in bathroom tubs. After a little discussion she agreed that fresh paint inside and out would make it seem brighter. I think she is concerned with her sister's health. She is not thinking long range for sure."

"I was afraid of that," Michael sighed. "She seems to be getting her house in order for all three of them to reach the end of the trail. I spoke to her about moving into an assisted living place and you would have thought she was about to slug me. They want to end their days right where they are. She did assure me that they have a very nice doctor who still makes house calls."

Michael, do you have any notion what you will do with 200 acres? Can some of it be sold off?"

He shrugged, "I haven't read the fine print, but all the conversation is that it must stay intact for another fifteen years, until the kids are adults. I suppose we could build houses to lease. But there have been no specifics; the whole area is zoned residential agriculture."

"Well, I've never seen better kept grape vines, that's for sure. They are old and well cared for. I'll bet that has been much of the income these ladies are using for living expenses, that and the cherries. The ladies must have some agreement with pickers because the day I went out to look at them there must have been thirty pickers taking care of the cherry harvest."

"I suppose I should have another meeting with Elva," Michael concluded, "to learn about those connections or learn about dreams they may have had for the place. I certainly don't want to move out there, but there is a certain charm about the whole place and an enormous amount of possibilities."

She snuggled against him in that welcomed way saying, "I had that water dream again. It seems like I am in a large room that is filling with water. I'm not cold or frightened and instead of numbers measuring the depth of the water there is only a sign that says 'enough'. What do you make of that dream?"

"I don't know" her happy husband said softly. "But I'm glad it doesn't panic you or disturb you in any way. Maybe it means you have to go potty."

Noell punched him with her elbow. "No I don't need a bathroom break. It is the same dream I have had for the last three nights."

Michael knew when his wife appreciated his humor and this wasn't one of those times. "I'm at a loss for an answer," he said simply. "But if there is one, I'll bet it makes itself clear in a day or two."

The breakfast dishes were just picked up when Ms. Chambers called. "Good morning. Sir. I hope I am not disturbing you. The ladies asked me to call early to make a lunch date for this afternoon. Ida has a doctor's appointment at two and we hoped you would ask Cheryl to save us four turkey sandwiches, six if you and Noell will join us. Ava and Elva would love to be able to listen to the orchestra rehearsal, and Elva believes you would like to chat with her about the property."

A little shiver ran up Michael's back. How could she know? "I'll make sure she saves us six. We would love to hear about some of the early dreams for the property." He took a breath and continued, "And Ms. Chambers, if you can find out about the land adjacent to ours on the north side, I'll have a retainer check for you as well."

"Goody, goody" she giggled. "I love new business, but I already know that Weyerhaeuser Timber owns a very large plot there. Do you mind telling me why you are interested."

"I have a buddy from the Corps who has always wanted to have a dance studio, but since he has two left feet, he'll settle for a winery. I just thought if we have grapes, he might dovetail into the development of something more."

Her happy voice said, "I'll look into it for you, pro bono. We'll see you about noon."

As he hung up the phone, Noell asked, "What in the world would you want with more property? You don't know what you are going to do with all that you already have."

"Right you are, just remember that I didn't know what I was going to do with this when we first looked into it. Noell, I have always considered information as neutral. It's what we do with it that gives it positive or negative value. I don't know if Randall would want to purchase some of this new property. But I would welcome him as a neighbor for sure. I don't know how much money he rescued. But I'll bet he still has enough to build a dream for himself." He raised his eyebrows and added, "Let's just see what we can learn today."

The ladies were all happy to be back in Harmony House. Before they were seated they embraced Noell and kissed Michael's hand. The first topic was their gratitude for the new kitchen range and microwave, which were almost as appreciated as the new walk-in bathtub. They nearly giggled with delight. Then they each shared their gratitude for gentle peace without Till's nuisance. The fresh paint almost removed the memories of Erma's death.

"Have any of your laborers returned, or is Daniel alone?" It was a subject that Michael had given considerable thought.

"Daniel is the only one there, but he still has family in Buena Vista. He returns home a couple times a month and his wife visits at least once a month. She helps us a lot then."

Michael asked for clarity, "Is it because the house he has is too small for his family?"

Ms. Chambers answered for them. "It is more the condition than size, but neither are adequate for a family. I also think that getting the children to school here would be a challenge. The nearest elementary school is in Gaston, six miles southeast of Cherry Grove."

"Well, if you once had seven workers, I have been thinking of a situation that might drastically improve the chances of building a small community. I have talked to the folks at Summit Construction who build offsite very nice three bedroom two bath homes that they can deliver to our foundations. They can place the first five here by the first of the month if we get a well dug. My offer to anyone whom Daniel approves is that they can pay $300 per month in rent and $50 in utilities from their wages. Anyone who remains for ten years gets to own the house."

Ms. Chambers stared at Michael and the other three wept. Elva said softly, "That is the most gracious proposal I have ever heard. To think that they could become homeowners is beyond belief for most workers. You have more than justified our choice in you." The other three nodded in agreement. "Till wanted our property because he did not have enough irrigation to accomplish his plan. He wanted to take our aquifer. But you have found a way to give it to those who will benefit from it."

Ms. Chambers scrunched her lips and said, "I don't want to pour cold water on a good moment but I did talk to the folks at Weyerhaeuser. They purchased the land when it appeared that our folks would grow large enough to block the timber company from the Tillamook forest west of here. They purchased three thousand acres just to build a road from our lane up to the forest service road. They will sell it to you for what they paid, $300 an acre if you will buy it all and give them a permanent easement and maintain the road in its present condition. Most of the property west of here is rocky as it goes up the hill, but north of here is very similar to the property we now have and it extends nearly a mile to Hagg Lake. You would have enough water to meet just about any need."

Noell said softly, "For the last three nights I have been dreaming of water, enough water. This is very strange."

Elva was smiling as she said, "Yes, in a very wonderful way. A seer would have received a sign and you did."

Michael added, "With that much property to work with we could have the winery for sure and a golf course and a bed and breakfast lodge near the lake. We could develop a bunch of home sites up the hill. I can imagine using this area in a very special way for a very long time. We just need to put the right people together with the right resources." He looked at Noell who was smiling brightly as she said, "And we have them both."

Michael also grinned as he concluded, "I'll wire transfer nine hundred thousand dollars to the Escrow people we used before and you can tell me how much the title insurance and transfer fee will be."

Ms. Chambers studied his face for a moment. It is easy to misread someone who can so casually move nearly a million dollars.

The rehearsal was over and the children were gone. Elva and Ada sat in the empty auditorium until Michael invited them to come into their home where they would be more comfortable. Noell was preparing a tasty stew that they could share. Lisle phoned to say the doctor was not ready to release Ida and they would be at Harmony House as soon as they could. An hour slid by with listening to the children practice and small talk, stories of the early days of Cherry Grove.

Finally Elva looked directly into Michael's eyes and said, "You have become like dear family to me, so let me tell you about Lisle. I know that you wonder how she fits into our story." She took a deep breath and began. "In 1936 I was a happy nineteen year old working at the marine supply near my father's police station. One afternoon a very handsome young man came in to purchase some equipment for the new boat they were moving from San Francisco to Port Hardy B.C.. He ask me if I could recommend any nearby restaurant and when I suggested a couple he asked which one would I choose to go with him. My father's shift was over at nine o'clock so I knew I had plenty of time, but not as much good sense."

"Scott was charming, delightfully witty and polite. I was smitten. He walked me to my father's station and said he hoped that we would see one another the next day. We were together all that day and when he once again politely walked me to the station he informed me that they were leaving in the morning. He would stop in to say goodbye to me. When that moment came, he asked me to accompany them on Capricious, an appropriate name for his boat. They were going to Port Hardy on the north end of Vancouver Island. My lips said that would be inappropriate but my heart wasn't listening. He said we could be married when the boat returned to Vancouver. I said I had no clothes. He pointed out a department store on the corner. I wrote Papa a brief note and followed my heart."

"We stopped in customs in Victoria. On the paper he filled in our names as Mr. and Mrs. Scott Chambers. We stopped for the night in Nanaimo, sleeping together in the captain's stateroom. The next day we stopped in Campbell river. He was gentle gracious and passionate. I was head over heels in love."

"The next morning we were lazy, staying under covers even when the skipper advised us to cast off with a rapidly ebbing tide." Her voice broke as she admitted, "We tarried. Once in the Seymour Narrows we could see the rapids and felt the violent current pushing the boat around. The ebbing tide had carried the water away that we needed to get safely across Ripple Rock. The collision was a nightmare. In fear I had found a place on the main deck near a life ring. When we hit the rock our boat split wide open. The current drug the lovely craft over the rock simply shredding Capricious into splinters. Scott was holding my hand one moment and the next I was alone in the swirling water. I saw no other swimmers."

"A nearby boat plucked me from the frigid water and wrapped me in a dry blanket. At the dock I told them I was from the Capricious out of Vancouver; we had entered at the Victoria customs. A Canadian Mounted Police car took me down island and then when they had an address for me, I was placed on a ferry to Vancouver where another Mounted Policeman met me and drove me to the Chambers' home. He was a Canadian timber baron. As you might expect there was considerable shouting and name-calling. All I could do was weep and tell them about the final days of their dear son's life. They angrily put me on a bus for Seattle with enough money to get to Portland. A girl on the bus shared her lunch with me."

"Again as you might suspect my father was furious with me. His silence was even worse than the Chambers' name calling. For nearly a month I was an outcast. Then I missed my monthly period. Father wrote a letter to the Chambers asking if they would honor their son by helping with my maternity expenses. A week before I was full term. Mrs. Chambers came to my Father's station asking if she could see me. It was a tearful moment. They had reconsidered their rejection of me. I would have their assistance if I would put Scott's name on the birth certificate, which I gladly did. Lisle Vera Chambers came into my life. They wanted me to bring her to Vancouver right away, instead they were regular visitors to Cherry Grove. When she was five the nation went to war. When she was seven she went to Vancouver for the summer and they came to Portland twice to visit. They declared that her eyes and smile were exactly that of their son; no clearer proof could demonstrate his presence. That was a regular pattern until she was in high school, then her trips north were cut back. Several universities offered her a scholarship but she stayed near home choosing to accept their offer to make her under graduate degree from the University of Oregon. Chambers offered her a couple years at Oxford, then she finished her law degree from Harvard believing that she wanted to work in the U.S. legal system."

"Mr. Chambers experienced a massive heart attack the year she was in Oxford. He passed away before she could come home to pray for him. Mrs. Chambers developed a terrible cancer that snuffed out her life in just a few months even with prayer. Lisle was named the sole heir of their vast estate. She liquidated everything and came back to Portland opening her own law firm. She has made sensible investments since then, except the limousines which she insists on owning and enjoys being driven."

"Wait a minute," Michael interrupted. "Are you telling us that Lisle Chambers is your seventy two year old daughter?" He seemed befuddled. "She looks and acts like a twenty two year old woman."

Elva nodded with understanding. "When she was in Harvard she stood in the center of the circle and received the blessings of the priestesses. In becoming one herself she has accepted a chaste life, never marrying. I think that is the reason she is so fond of your family. You are allowing her to vicariously enjoy the wonder of raising children. Be careful, she will do her best to spoil them."

Just then the double door bells rand. It was Lisle explaining that Ida had been admitted to the hospital. Her nagging illness was finally diagnosed as pneumonia and she was resting comfortably now on oxygen.

Noell stood up and gave her a hug saying, "We were just about to share some stew and Lazy-girl corn bread. Will you join us, please?" It may have been the result of the lingering embrace, or perhaps it was the "please" or then there might have been the memories of a star circle. Lisle agreed that it would be very pleasant to share their table.

Most of the conversation at dinner focused on the possibilities in the new acquisition. Michael's idea of a golf course was questioned at first because it is a long drive from Portland. But when he pointed out that being on the lee side of the coastal range it would have dryer weather than most courses and the possibility of a bed and breakfast lodge would offer an attraction, he had new believers. Noell said the availability of Hagg Lake might be attractive to fishermen. Lisle surprised everyone by saying that she had always wanted a weekend house away from the city, with a barn where she could raise Cleveland Bay broodmares. Their characteristic deep red color with black legs, mane and tail would be a welcomed sight pulling a carriage in the Rose Parade.

Elva said she couldn't get the image out of her mind of several nice homes for the workers. She thought that with grapes and cherries, a winery, a golf course and a bed and breakfast there would be employment for several new families. Her smile was the warmest at the table, a fact not lost to Michael.

"I talked with Kenny today who told me that he had a well driller lined up for the weekend, and would begin removing some of those unusable buildings and the barn. He also has contacted a surveyor to set clear boundaries, which will be especially important now with additional land. I've also been in contact with the phone company who would be very happy to place a cell phone tower on an out-of-the-way corner somewhere."

Looking again at Elva he asked, "We're going to need a manager who might have contacts in the labor force. Will you speak to Daniel for me? I'm thinking that he might be a genuine asset as we get this rolling along. In fact, do you agree that this has been a fruitful meeting?" When everyone nodded he suggested, "Perhaps every Tuesday we could have an afternoon information time. That way Lisle won't need a special excuse to enjoy another of Cheryl's yummy sandwiches." There were smiles all around so he concluded, "It's been moved, seconded, and unanimously carried to make Tuesday noon our Cherry Grove Enhancement meeting. Cheryl will reserve our table and six sandwiches and I'll pick up the tab."

Aren't dreams amazing? They are more delicate than a cobweb and more persistent than a planter's wart. They are so fleeting that in the morning they may leave only a wistful hint of information you try to retrieve or so engrossing you can think of little else for hours because they haunt you so. Kenny took the plans of six Summit Construction homes to the Yamhill County Planning, explaining that they were simply replacing the eye-sores that had been torn down. Within a week he had permits to build. He took the concept drawing of a winery and a Summit Construction Tillamook style house and with a successful perk test was given two more permits. He took the concept drawing of an eight stall barn and another Tillamook style home design. And they didn't even ask for a perk test, he was given the permit. Dreams have a fleeting duration, or a lingering tenacity. June turned into July and then August and the children of Harmony House had a banner summer of music making.

By the first of September the roads were defined with yellow flags, the homes established and the first families arriving. Sadly Ida did not get to see any of it. Her dream was complete and her ashes scattered on the hillside above the land that she had loved all her days. Some would say that dreams are only fantasy, but others contend they are the reality that exists between the labors of daylight hours. Elva relinquished her life gently and before the autumn solstice, so did Ada. The dreamers of the past stepped off their stage, and those of the future endured the bright lights of the present.

Randall looked at Michael impatiently saying, "No man, I'm not kidding. My vintner has said this is an ideal eco-zone to grow Viognier grapes. We planted the two hundred original acres with Chardonnay, but this is more rocky. It's drier and they will make terrific wine. I'm serious. I'll pay you for all the land you have up this hillside."

Michael had tried to explain that facing east it would get great morning sun but little in the afternoon and on the lee side of the hill there would be little rain. He wondered if Randall was getting rid of his confiscated cash too, but finally said, "O.K. I look forward to some of this fractured wine."

At the same time Mr. Klein was making an unusual request to Noell. "The principle violinist with Riverdance has battled with Arthritis for months. Now on tour she is playing more than ever and aggravated both hands. Will you bring the girls and their violins to the Orpheum?" When Noell asked if he meant right now, the director said, "If she doesn't get some relief, she may not be able to play the show tonight. I know it is a long shot, but I feel it's the only thing we haven't tried."

Twenty minutes later Cele and Cam were in Ms. Nesbitt's dressing room tuning the violins. The nine note chord was played twice and then they played a selection from the Celtic fiddles, much to the artist's entertainment. When they were finished they played their tuning chord again, twice.

When the Riverdance show was over, the principle violinist assured her manager that there wasn't a sign of discomfort in her hands or wrists. She attested the change to a restful afternoon. The children were already out of her memory. But the three gratis tickets that had been provided to Noell and the girls left a deep memory of style and perfection by the violinist they had cheered. Dreams are fleeting or life changing at times.

Paul had passed his third year med exams and with the approval of the VA had been working full shifts in the Legacy Trauma center. His colleagues saw his skill and devotion to the job as an enormous asset. Many were surprised when they learned about his extensive battle wounds. His energy level and freedom from lingering signs were amazing to them. Noell had helped him buy a new car so he didn't need to depend upon others driving him to the hospital. It was his housing situation that was a nagging point.

"I know I have way over-stayed my welcome here," he had admitted. "If it weren't for Gabe I'd get my own place near the hospital. That would be best for all of us, except him. This is the perfect place for him and I can't imagine being away from him more than necessary."

Noell and Michael both assured him that there was no need to make other arrangements. It was all good right now. They loved Gabe and even more loved seeing how disciplined Paul had been in reaching toward his goal.

An early November snow fall on Mt. Hood had the skiing community thrilled. Timberline opened a couple weeks earlier than ever before and the national team trials were set for the first of the month. Sarah Laven was excited with her new Atomic GS skies. Nine centimeters longer than her old ones but with a new radial side-cut they would be more maneuverable. It was too bad that she couldn't put new bindings on at the same time, but her old ones were still in great shape. After the first two trial runs she was in the top thirty.

An enormous bouquet of flowers accompanied by a basket of seasonal goodies was delivered to Harmony Home in care of the "Amazing violin duet that saved my life." The note that accompanied it said, "I still remember the frightening moments before the violins came to my rescue. I still don't understand how it worked, but I continue to enjoy good health and tender thoughts of your mercy. The enclosed check is a donation to the Aloha Youth Symphony. If you forward me the dates of their programs, I will be in the front row." It was signed by Jed and Jess Phipps.

Her first run of the morning had been in the top twenty; she was convinced she could improve on the time. Her second run was up with the leaders and she knew she had a better one still for her final trial run. It had taken all year to strengthen her quads and knees, now she was grateful for the effort. The Giant Slalom was not only a test of skiing skill it was a brutal test of strength. She kicked out of the starting gate and dropped into a tight tuck as her speed increased. Gate one went past in a blur; two and three were well under control. But she was late on four which made her wide on five. Sarah knew she had to cut these next four gates close; they were crucial. She hooked gate seven with her right ski and felt her entire body snap around in a nightmare crash. Her binding did not release and she went airborne backwards. The searing pain in her knee and thigh screamed that she had a serious injury, or was that scream from her terrified voice. She doesn't remember the impact that finally released both skies, nor the tumbling crash that covered about a hundred meters of mountainside until fortunately her unconscious body came to rest in a safety net.

Ski Patrol folks were there within a couple minutes and a sled was there nearly as soon. An unconscious Sarah was immobilized for a rescue sled to the bottom of the run and a helicopter transfer to Good Samaritan Hospital in Portland. The severity of her head and neck injuries had to be determined before they could consider the orthopedics. Fortunately an intern by the name of Paul Frost was on duty.

While the initial X-rays were being examined he convinced his lead physician to examine her knee. It would be impossible to stabilize the upper leg, which had a spiral fracture, without doing some repair to the knee. It was easy to see that in the past she had already had two meniscus repairs. There was very little of it left. Dr. Jeffries was dubious at first, but then agreed it would be best to try a simple implant procedure rather than schedule a full knee replacement. Since she needed no anesthesia, it took them less than twenty minutes to clean out the tattered meniscus and insert a Peterson Pad. Paul had been convincing when he affirmed that he was wearing one of those now himself. He then suggested that an air splint with a 45 degree anterior twist would hold her leg stable until they could give it full attention.

The severe concussion was most worrisome. There was obvious swelling of the brain and her neck had sustained a major sprain. That also remained stabilized and the waiting began.

The following day there was no change in Sarah's condition. Perhaps the swelling was increasing, which was not a good sign. A procedure to drain off some of that fluid was scheduled for tomorrow.

At dinner Paul was telling the folks about a skier who was in bad shape. He called her by name, Sarah.

"By any chance would that be Sarah Laven" Michael asked even though he was wondering how many Sarah's lived in Portland.

"Why yes it is," a surprised Paul answered. "How in the world would you know that?"

"She did the translation of the old manuscripts we found on the front part of the property. With the gratuity I gave her she said she was going to get some new speedy skies. She is a super nice lady and really bright. She has a doctorate and teaches languages at Portland State."

Paul explained the severity of her injuries and her coma state. He had been told stories of marvelous recovery that included the violins in ways unfamiliar to his extensive experience or study. But he was hesitant to ask. If anything could help this patient he was willing to try it. But he didn't know how to ask.

"Oh for goodness sake," Noell said softly. "You just say, 'I have a patient that needs your help girls. Do you have a couple minutes to try?' That's how you ask."

A shocked brother looked at her and said "Do you read minds or was my expression that obvious? I'm supposed to be a doctor and your stories are outside the boundary of modern medicine."

"It's visiting hour at the hospital isn't it?" Noell said with a confident smile. "I need to make a phone call and then we can head over there. What is Sarah's room number? Girls get your coats and violins."

Michael's grin was pure joy because he knew three things: that he could stay home with Gabe; Paul was in for one big puzzle; Sarah was in for serious assistance.

Lisle was waiting outside the room for them. A couple nurses were confused when a group came in to see Sarah, but since Dr. Frost accompanied them it had to be O.K. Inside the room they found Sarah's mom Jenny sitting quietly beside her still daughter. Tubes and wires were attached and a machine was assisting her breathing. The startled mom stood until Paul explained that this small prayer group knew of Sarah's work with students and wanted to help. She sat down as the girls opened their violin cases and softly played a nine note tuning cord, then remaining in that soft volume they played "*It Is Well with My Soul.*" They played the tuning chord again, twice and placed the violins back in their cases. Noell asked Jenny to hold Sarah's hand while Lisle held the other. She held Lisle's hand and asked Paul to hold Jenny's and her hands. Even though one was a male, they had a star circle and there was power in it. She prayed, "Mighty and Gracious God, in this tender time we seek your comfort upon Sarah, your healing and strength. We recall that her name means laughter. Let her dance before you as a happy well woman. In the name of Jesus the Great Healer we ask this. Amen"

Now how long did that take? Maybe seven minutes tops and yet for years to come those short minutes would affect many. Jenny had felt it, a burst of light that went through them. She experienced the healing power of the Holy Spirit herself, and no one would convince her differently!

Lisle felt it and it confirmed the wisdom of her mother in choosing Noell as Compassion. There was hope for the Oskimey.

Paul had felt a surge of healing power unlike that of the medical books. He was confident that Sarah was going to be well. He also had a fresh respect and admiration for his sister who was forever a surprise to him.

Noell had felt the bolt of power generated by the circle. She felt a new intense affection for Lisle and Paul, but also for Jenny and Sarah. They were welded together now with an unbreakable bold.

Sarah felt it. The violins had sounded far away at first. Their melody told her that her injuries were not permanent, she would recover. She wanted to open her eyes and see these marvelous people who had awakened her. But for the moment, she could not. However, she was confident that the emptiness in her heart was about to be filled to overflowing and she was ready.

Think about that! In just seven minutes all heaven broke loose and it brought them all a fresh dream of the future.

Carrey James missed the Saturday afternoon rehearsal for the church service. When Caleb shared that information with his mom, Noell called Karen. She was told that Carrey's cold had turned into a hacking cough and then a pretty bad fever. "The doctor has prescribed some antibiotics that should help," Mrs. James reported. "I'm sure it is just one of those kid things that will be gone in the morning. Thanks for your concern."

But when the family was absent from the church service, Noell called again and learned that Carrey's temperature had gone up to 105° during the night and they had taken her to Dornbecker Children's Hospital.

Later that afternoon an alarmed Rusty called to report that Carrey was nonresponsive to the doctors and her family was asking for prayers from the congregation for his very sick daughter. Noell's response was to call Lisle, and Cheryl. She asked them to meet her at the Children's hospital right away. Then she asked the twins to get their coats and violins. Caleb offered to accompany them, but was asked to stay home and pray for his friend.

The hospital hallways were pretty empty now that visiting hours were over. The nurse that greeted them was told that the family had requested prayer. "We'll be less than ten minutes," Noell promised. "Then we will leave quietly." She directed them to the room where anxious parents waited helplessly.

Noell knocked softly on the door and went in, immediately embracing Karen and Rusty, both of whom had tears on their face. "We brought a little more prayer power," she said to her friends. "The girls wouldn't be satisfied until we came to the assistance of their best friend." The violins were already out of their cases and playing their tuning chord. They played one verse of *Sweet Hour of Prayer* then played their tuning chord twice again. Noell suggested that Karen hold Carrey's hand and Rusty hold the other. Lisle joined the chain of prayer as did Cheryl then Noell held Cheryl's and Rusty's hands. "We are five in prayer," she said bowing her head. "Heavenly Lord of Wonder, we repeat the words of Jesus when he healed a little girl simply by saying 'Arise'. We are confident that healing and health is now pouring into Carrey, overcoming the sickness and restoring her wonderful body. In the name of Christ the Healer we seek your healing Mercy. Amen."

Was there a flash of power? No. It was more like a grateful surge of confidence, faith that Carrey's condition was improving by the minute, which it was.

After embraces all around, the team was on its way out the front door when Noell stopped them and said to Cheryl, "I counted on your friendship to help us and you really did. We have recently lost three prayer warriors. I'm going to ask you later what you saw and felt just now because I believe you will become a replacement. We must be five. Thank you. She gave Cheryl a hug as did Lisle, who had been a fascinated observer again. Then she thanked the twins for being such good warriors too.

Before they separated to their individual cars, Lisle asked Noell, "I'm thrilled that you are thinking about replacements. Do you believe that Cheryl might consider a consecrated life?" Her eyes searched Noell's

"We'll see," she answered. "I also think Karen could and Sarah as well. There is no rush. We simply must remain faithful. The circle will choose the right ones."

Doctor Paul was making his evening rounds of post op patients. Everyone except Ms. Laven was showing signs of recovery. He stood at the foot of her bed checking the numbers; respiration was unchanged; pulse was unchanged; temperature was normal. He wondered if that head injury was deeper than they first thought. He felt her toes to see if they were still cold and clammy.

"That really tickles," he heard her say softly.

"Welcome back, ma'am," he said in an equally soft voice. "We have been pretty worried about you. I'm Paul Frost intern here at Legacy Good Samaritan. You took a nasty crash at the ski trials and have been unconscious for two and a half days. Can you tell me of any pain you have right now?"

"I have a little bit of a headache and my neck is sort of sore," she said in a clearer voice. "Mom was here, and my boyfriend, when the violins were played. I tried to open my eyes to see them and I couldn't." She was still for a moment. "Doctor this is really strange. I don't feel like I was in a crash, and I'm pretty sure I don't have a boyfriend."

Paul chuckled, "You slammed into that icy mountain at seventy five miles an hour. I'm sure things are going to be scrambled for a bit. Dr. Jeffries is your attending physician. He'll be glad to hear that you are back with us. Can you open your eyes for me?"

There was a lengthy pause and she replied, "Nope. I can't seem to find the switch. Could I please have a sip of water instead?"

As he lifted the glass he said, "Here comes the straw. Just take small sips."

She drank about half the glass. Apparently she was thirsty. "Mmm thank you." There was a brief pause as she took a deep breath, and then she said in a near whisper, "That's a nice fragrance you are wearing." She sighed and her body relaxed.

Paul smiled because hospital policy is fragrance neutral for both doctors and nurses. It was hard to tell but he thought she had gone back to sleep.

The following afternoon as Paul began his shift, he went first to Sarah's room. He found Dr. Jeffries and a nurse reviewing her clipboard. When the doctor looked up he said, "I thought you reported that she regained consciousness. So far today there has been no...."

"Doctor Frost." Sarah said softly, "I was just thinking about you. Good morning."

Paul stepped up to the bed and held her hand. "Good morning Sarah. How are you feeling today?" Dr. Jeffries and the nurse moved a bit closer to the patient.

"I feel rested and still pretty fuzzy about the crash. I sure hope I didn't damage those new skies. They are hot." She hadn't yet opened her eyes.

"Sarah, can you open your eyes for me?" Paul asked. "I'd like to check that concussion."

With a cheery half smile, her blue eyes opened and she said, "You still smell really nice."

Doctor Jeffries moved a bit closer and sniffed. He could detect no unauthorized fragrance on his intern. "Nurse Connors," he directed. "would you go out into the waiting room and tell Mrs. Laven that Sarah has regained consciousness?" Then he looked at his patient and said, "Ms. Laven, I'm Dr. Jeffries, your Orthopedist. Our initial exam showed extensive damage to your knee and femur. Are you seriously in no discomfort?" He was baffled by her apparent comfort with little medication.

Softly she said, "I'm smart enough not to play jokes on the one who is trying to comfort me. Truly, I feel like I should just get up and go home." Her mom hurried into the room and went straight to Sarah, holding her hand and kissing her cheek,

"I just knew the Holy Spirit was bringing you healing and strength," her mom whispered. "We prayed and God answered. Thank you Jesus!"

The Youth Symphony Christmas sing-a-long was a huge success. They had requests for the free tickets that filled the auditorium on two nights. It was more than anyone could imagine. Once again Mr. Klein distributed T-shirts, these green with white letters and red with white letters for the second night. As the second night folks were cheerily exiting Michael and Noell were in the foyer chatting with folks. There were so many who wanted to thank them or compliment the youth program.

A patient lady with a daughter stood by the wall waiting for an opportunity to speak with them. Finally there was enough of a lull that she stepped up to Michael and offered her hand saying, "This was an amazing evening! I haven't had this much Christmas spirit since I was a little girl. I'm Crystal Meyers."

Michael smiled broadly and said, "This is our first attempt at a sing-along and it worked out much better than expected." Looking at the young girl he asked, "Who is this young lady?"

"This is Julie. She was blown away by how many talented kids were here. Are any of them yours?"

Noell answered, "The young man on the piano is Caleb, and the first and second violins are Cam and Cele. They are ours."

Michael asked Julie, "Do you play an instrument? Would you like to be a part of the orchestra?"

Crystal chuckled, "She would love to be able to take lessons, but we don't have a piano."

She might have said more but Michael asked, "You look real familiar to me. This is my wife Noell. Have we met before?"

"I've heard I look a lot like my mom. I think you knew her. But we were just kids." When he shook his head in confusion, she continued, "In the birth order I was in the middle. I was a trouble maker for a while. There were a few rehabs and four years in Monroe. Then I met Bruce Meyers who was a helicopter pilot in Iraq. We were married long enough to have Jewels, who we call Julie. When he was killed I used the insurance money to go to school. Now I'm the director of the South Cowlitz Women's Shelters."

Michael was processing all this information more slowly than it was coming at him. He was wondering why this woman was trying so hard to get her daughter into the Aloha program.

Crystal shrugged in frustration. "I have an older brother who lives in the Portland area and a younger brother who lives in a mansion in Seattle. Stars and little fishes, I don't know how to make it much clearer without spilling everything. Seven years ago you guys each put a snow job on the other. You accepted the notion that he was a custodian in an AIDs clinic, and he thought you were some hairy street bum trying to hustle some cash. There went another decade of family. My birth name was Chrissy. Which I changed when I married Bruce. For Crying out loud, I'm your sister."

While that was soaking in, Noell hugged her sincerely. "Oh Sweetie, I've never had a sister!" she said with a sob. "Thank you for finding us."

Michael wrapped his arms around both of them and said, "Stars and little fishes, we have a lot of catching-up to do. I know a winemaker who would love to meet you"

Finis: Now There Are Five!

Printed in the United States
By Bookmasters